"IF HE MOVES HIS HEAD AT ALL, BLOW HIS BRAINS OUT."

Montsero did as he was told. As he felt the cold metal touch the back of his neck, Chant flexed his knees slightly and watched with the other men as Hammerhead slowly came down into the well, stopped in front of him.

There was nothing Chant could do as the hand with the gun suddenly shot out and the barrel slammed into the side of his head, just above the temple.

Chant tried to kick at the other man, but the strength in his legs was gone. He put his hands to his head, then sank slowly down into a vast sea of shimmering, orange-streaked pain...

CHANT

Code of Blood

DAVID CROSS

A JOVE BOOK

CHANT: CODE OF BLOOD

A Jove Book/published by arrangement with
the author

PRINTING HISTORY
Jove edition/January 1987

ISBN: 0-515-08886-2

Jove Books are published by The Berkley Publishing Group,
200 Madison Avenue, New York, N.Y. 10016.
The words "A JOVE BOOK" and the "J" with sunburst
are trademarks belonging to Jove Publications, Inc.

PRINTED IN THE UNITED STATES OF AMERICA

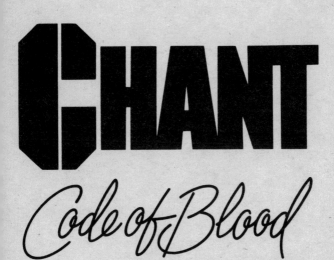

CHANT
Code of Blood

the run _____

With Montsero offering a thousand dollars in bonus money to the winner, and with no rules except that the winner would be the first to cross the finish line, Chant had anticipated that there would be a lot of kicking, swinging of fists and elbows in the tightly packed starting area. Intent on masking the range of his skills from Montsero whenever possible, Chant had avoided initial physical combat by actually stepping back and to the side when Montsero had dropped his arm to signal the start of the cross-country run. As the others, cursing and swinging at one another, scrambled away, Chant unhurriedly removed his boots and socks and tossed them to the side.

Montsero grunted with surprise. "You're not running on the beach at Acapulco, Alter. Your feet will freeze in this weather, if you don't break a couple of toes."

Chant merely smiled at the renegade psychologist, then started off at an easy trot after the others as the leaders disappeared over the crest of a small hill two hundred yards away.

Chant loped at an easy pace until he was over the hill, out

of Montsero's sight, then abruptly broke into a seiki-kwa style of running designed for moving with fluid grace and considerable speed over rough terrain. Within a minute after shifting to seiki-kwa motion he had caught and passed the last runner besides himself at the back of the group. Chant silently shot past him, and the man could do nothing but stare in astonishment after the big man who seemed not so much to run as to float, his bare feet hardly seeming to touch the sharp rocks or frozen, rutted ground over which he passed.

The next five men were bunched together on the far side of a steep embankment leading down to a frozen stream; unwilling to risk breaking a leg by walking or running down the hill, the men were negotiating the descent on their backsides. Chant paused for just a moment at the top of the hill to gauge his own angle of descent, grinned with pleasure at the challenge offered by the precipitous slope, then leaped headfirst out into the freezing air. He hit the first patch of ice-encrusted snow on his left shoulder and rolled, coming up on his feet and immediately springing out into the air once again. In this way, by literal leaps and bounds, Chant flew down the steep embankment.

Sometimes it appeared that he must collide with one of the numerous outcroppings of sharp rock, but at the last moment he always glided just past or above them. An observer would have considered Chant's headlong plunge down the steep, boulder-strewn slope suicidal, but in fact he was enjoying himself immensely, reveling in the sensation of flight through the cold air. All of his senses were finely focused on, tuned to, his surroundings, and his body had become not an opponent of, but part of the earth over which he traveled with such seemingly effortless grace and speed. This blood test, he thought, was perfect for his immediate purpose—which was not to win the race (which he knew he would), but to practice his very special mental and physical skills.

Within five minutes he had caught the leader; the man who had sprinted out ahead of the pack at the beginning was just ahead of Chant, virtually exhausted but plodding on nonethe-

less. Sensing rather than hearing Chant coming up behind him, the man stopped and turned, his face flushing with consternation and rage. With Chant barely twenty-five yards away, the man picked up a sharp-edged rock and flung it at Chant, who plucked the rock out of the air and, without breaking stride, flicked his wrist and flung the rock back at the man with the speed and power of a major league catcher firing a ball to second base. The man cried out in surprise and barely managed to duck in time as the rock whistled through the air over his head.

Obviously baffled by Chant's speed and reflexes but still enraged by the thought that he could lose the race and bonus money, the ex-convict picked up a heavy, dead branch from the ground and, cocking it like a baseball bat, moved threateningly into Chant's path. However, at the last moment the ex-convict thought better of attacking this strange, quiet man who had nearly killed him with his return throw of the rock; he dropped the branch, then quickly backed away as Chant loped past without even glancing at him.

Alone, comfortably ahead of the others, Chant stopped and glanced around him. Throughout the run he had been occasionally bothered by the feeling that he was being watched— not by the ex-convicts, who were for the most part unobservant, inarticulate and respectful only of strength, will, and ruthlessness, but by someone else. The men pitted against him in these trials would be impressed only with what he did, not by how he did it; they would take no notice of the techniques of seiki-kwa, would care only that he had somehow managed to best them.

Montsero, or another trained observer watching him from a distance, could be quite another matter.

Chant finished the run, without employing seiki-kwa, and as he crossed the finish line pretended to be much more tired than he actually was.

CHAPTER ONE ⸻

IT WAS A typically cold, rainy English day but in the great library of the Elizabethan manor that belonged to the man known as Sir Gerald Coughlin, a bright, cheerful fire burned. In an armchair by the fire sat a towering man with iron-colored eyes and close-cropped, iron-colored hair.

Few here in England knew the true identity of this man, who years before in Vietnam had been Captain John Sinclair and was now known more frequently to both friends and enemies simply as Chant. John Sinclair was the Most Wanted Man on the hit lists of everyone from the CIA and the KGB to Interpol and the FBI, not to mention a hundred or so local police departments around the world. He therefore found it preferable while in England to pose as wealthy and influential Sir Gerald Coughlin.

The man who fussed with a pile of newspaper clippings on a desk in one corner of the room was one of the few who knew all of Chant's real identities; he was Alistair Powers, valet, butler, chauffeur, personal secretary, and researcher to Chant.

It was his duty to collect file clippings from newspapers around the world, collate information, and suggest possible future operations. At this moment, he was in the process of winding up the paperwork on a successful operation Chant had recently finished—eliminating an old-age-home scam in Florida.

As Alistair worked, he would occasionally glance up idly at the television near his desk, whose images flickered silently on an all-news channel. He was about to look away, when a picture on the silent screen caught his eye—and suddenly he felt his breath catch in his throat. He just managed to stifle an exclamation of shock and sorrow.

On the screen, in stark close-up, was the bloody, bullet-riddled body of a gray-haired, aristocratic-looking man whose face was now clenched in a grotesque death grimace. It was a face Alistair knew very well, for he had admitted the man many times through the gates of this very house—served him drinks and dinner, talked with him. It was the face of a man who had known Alistair's secrets, as well as John Sinclair's, and whom Alistair had liked very much.

The camera slowly panned a few feet away to the corpse of a second, bearded man dressed in ragged clothes, and Alistair received his second shock.

Alistair knew that his employer, whose back was to the television, could not see the images on the screen, and he quickly turned up the volume on the set, rather than waste any time alerting Chant. The camera cut to a montage of Rome.

"—*after pursuing some of the most powerful and dangerous men in Europe, there is perhaps more than a touch of terrible and bitter irony in the fact that Vito Biaggi finally met his death at the hands of a down-and-out, crazed American ex-convict who undoubtedly did not even know who Vito Biaggi was. In what Italian authorities agree was a senseless killing—*"

There were a few minutes more of the same, but the newscast was nearly finished, and the television soon switched to coverage of the busy London social scene. Alistair looked up from the television to see Chant once more staring into the fire, but he knew that his employer had heard and seen the shocking news. He sat back himself and stared at the ornate ceiling as his mind turned back to the bloody images on the television set, the announcer's voice, and thoughts of the gentle, bearish Italian magistrate who had been one of the few people entrusted with secrets that could destroy and kill John Sinclair.

Alistair had never understood the process by which his employer chose the men and women he would confide in. There were large rewards offered by organizations on both sides of the law for information leading to the capture, or death, of John Sinclair; yet he, with what seemed to Alistair casual disregard for his own safety, continued to offer to certain people he had decided to trust the secret of his real identity. Alistair, of course, was one of the select few, yet he did not understand why he had been chosen. He knew only that John Sinclair had changed his life, given him more than he had ever hoped to have in his life, and that he would gladly give his life for the enigmatic man with the iron-colored eyes and hair who offered life and justice to some, while delivering quick, often gruesome, death to others.

Alistair had never been told how John Sinclair and Vito Biaggi, a man sworn to uphold the law, had become friends. He did know that the Italian magistrate had been involved for more than a year in an intense and thorough investigation which attempted to unmask the identities of certain Europeans he suspected of channeling funds through Italian banks to terrorist groups around the world. Alistair also knew that the information Biaggi had acted upon in launching his investigation had been provided by John Sinclair, who had unearthed it in the course of an unrelated operation. The document John Sinclair had found and given to Vito Biaggi had hinted at the existence of an international cabal of amoral, apolitical businessmen who, in an attempt to purchase a kind of "terrorist insurance," provided a significant amount of funds to both left- and right-wing terrorist groups, in exchange for assurances that, in the event of the overthrow of certain governments, the interests of the funders would not be harmed.

Patiently but persistently, the Roman magistrate had taken the kernels of information that John Sinclair had provided and doggedly investigated, piecing together more bits of information and tracking down rumors. Only three weeks before, Vito Biaggi had announced that he could prove the existence of a global conspiracy that had already cost the lives of hundreds of people; indictments were imminent, and Biaggi had warned that the names of some very prominent people in the European Common Market would eventually surface.

Now, Alistair thought, Vito Biaggi was dead, at the hands of an expatriate street criminal; the Italian had been hunting monsters in the European forests, and he'd been killed by a maggot that had crawled out of the American criminal justice system, a man Alistair had once known.

Alistair sat still for a long while, then finally broke the silence. "Do you want me to make arrangements for you to attend Mr. Biaggi's funeral, sir?"

"I'm not going to the funeral," Chant said softly as he looked up from the fire. "You'll extend my regrets to Bianca, and tell her that I'll be in touch. I'm going to make some inquiries into Vito's death, and I want to start before too much time passes."

"Sir, I know the man who shot Mr. Biaggi."

The iron-colored eyes flicked in Alistair's direction. "Where do you know him from?"

"His name was Tyrone Good, and we were in San Quentin together. He was a lifer, like me, and we must have been together fifteen, sixteen years."

"Were you friends?" Chant asked evenly.

"Not likely. Good was a real pain in the ass; we just shared the same prison, and it's pretty hard in prison for long-termers not to get to know each other. He must have been paroled six or seven months after I was, and he must have heard of the Fortune Society in New York City. That's where I saw him again, at one of their meetings. It was just a few months after that when you—" Alistair turned away and wiped at his eyes; it was impossible for the old man to speak of what John Sinclair had done for him without tears coming to his eyes.

"Go on, Alistair," Chant said softly.

Alistair swallowed hard, found his voice. "There really isn't anything else. After you wiped out the Salieri family and saved my granddaughter from them, you asked if I'd like to come and work for you. I never saw Tyrone Good again. That was better than two years ago."

"Was this Tyrone Good Mafia?"

Alistair shook his head. "No way. I know what you're thinking; that the people Mr. Biaggi wanted to nail might have hired a hitter to kill him. Tyrone Good wouldn't have been the man; too stupid. You saw yourself: he got himself blown away."

"Indeed," Chant said in a slightly distant tone. "It would take a monumentally stupid man—"

"That was Tyrone."

"—to try and rob another man on the street in broad daylight, when the man was surrounded by three or four bodyguards."

Alistair nodded. "When I say Good was stupid, Mr. Sinclair, I mean like retarded. He also had a mean streak a mile wide, real psycho. After all the years I spent in San Quentin, I know something about Mafia types; some of them may be stupid, but they're highly disciplined—and they're not suicidal. I don't think Good was working for anyone, Mr. Sinclair. He was crazy, and he just did a crazy thing."

Chant sipped thoughtfully at his coffee. "And what do you suppose this crazy man was doing in Rome?" he asked softly.

Alistair thought about it, shook his head. "Good question, Mr. Sinclair. I don't think Tyrone even knew there was such a place as Europe, and if he had there would have been no reason for him to go there. As a matter of fact, I can't imagine where the hell he got the money; he was on welfare when I saw him in New York, and the only time I ever knew him to have more than five bucks in his pocket was when he and I both picked up a quick C-note by taking part in some weird college research project where they were studying ex-convicts." Alistair paused, again shook his head. "How Good got to Rome is a puzzle, all right, but I still don't see him being hired as a hitter by anyone who could afford better—and, from what I understand, the people Mr. Biaggi was after can afford to hire the best. Besides, Tyrone had his share of street smarts; he'd kill anyone for the fillings in their teeth—but not if there was a chance he'd be killed. I still think he just wigged out."

"Alistair," Chant asked slowly, "do you know, or have you ever heard of, a man by the name of Axle Trent?"

"Nope, can't say that I have. Who's Axle Trent?"

"Another American ex-convict. Seven months ago, in Geneva, Trent shot down a British diplomat who was a key figure in ongoing truce negotiations between two warring factions in the Sudan. Like Good, Axle Trent took it into his head to try to mug his victim in broad daylight, on a busy street; the police considered Trent, like Good, a most unlikely assassin, and they wrote off the murder as a senseless act by a psychopath with a long record of violent behavior."

"Was this Trent killed by the police?"

"He bashed out his own brains on the bars of his holding cell an hour after he was arrested. The police never found his passport, and nobody could explain what he was doing in Geneva. I remember the incident, because I happened to be in Geneva at the time; the killing was widely publicized."

"You think there could be a connection, sir?"

"I'm not sure yet," Chant said slowly, and lapsed back into silence, staring intently into the fire.

Alistair knew better than to interrupt him.

Finally Chant looked up again. "I'll be flying to New York tonight," he said. "Can you call British Airways and arrange for tickets?"

"I'll do that, sir, and I'll also call Mrs. Biaggi for you, as you asked."

Chant nodded. "Express condolences for both of us, tell

her I'm sorry I can't be with her right now. She'll understand. Don't mention anything about our conversation concerning Tyrone Good and Axle Trent."

"You're going to New York to talk to Tony Black, aren't you?"

Again, Chant nodded. "Yes, I am, Alistair," he said. "Thanks for all your help. You did well noticing that news broadcast when you did. I trust you to do all that's right in Italy."

"Thank you sir," said the old man, quietly and with dignity.

CHAPTER TWO ──────────

HIS LEGS ALWAYS hurt in cold, wet weather—the legacy of an old prison injury—and Tony Black paused at his desk to reach down and massage his thighs. After a minute or two the pain began to ease, and he went back to the pile of paperwork on his desk—applications for state and federal funding grants, correspondence with prisoners, requests for information and interviews, all the kinds of administrative details the ex-convict had learned to cope with since he had assumed the post of President of the Fortune Society almost a decade before.

He had not heard the downstairs door open, nor footsteps on the wooden stairway leading up to his second-floor office. However, suddenly he felt a presence in the room with him. He looked up and was mildly startled to see a big man, with longish red hair and a thick, droopy mustache, leaning in the doorway, looking at him. The man wore a three-quarter-length gabardine topcoat against the December chill, and in his right hand he held a sturdy walnut cane. Black leaned back in his swivel chair, ran the fingers of his left hand through his thin-

ning blond hair, pushed his thick bifocals up on the bridge of
his nose, and stared back at the man. He knew no one with
fiery red hair who walked with a cane, but there was something about the presence of this big man with the thick
shoulders, slim waist, and powerful thighs that seemed familiar.

"That you, Chant?"

Chant smiled, put aside the cane, and walked across the
office. "Hello, Tony. How are you?"

Black rose, hurried around the desk, and embraced the man
with whom he shared a friendship that had begun in the
blood-soaked jungles of Vietnam. *"Damn, Chant, it's good to
see you."*

"And you, Tony. How are the legs?"

"They hurt like hell in weather like this, but just the sight
of you makes them feel better. It's been a long time, my
friend. Too long."

"Agreed."

"You want a drink?"

"You still have my bottle?"

'Of course I still have your bottle. It's been sitting there
gathering dust since the last time you were in the city."

"It only improves with age."

Tony Black limped across the room, closed the office door,
and pulled a shade down over the window. Then he went to a
large filing cabinet, opened the bottom drawer, and took out a
bottle of Scotch and one of fine, imported saki. He removed a
tiny china cup from a plastic bag, filled it with saki. Holding
the cup by its rim with his fingertips, he passed the flame of a
cigarette lighter four times across its bottom before handing it
to Chant, who accepted the cup with a slight bow from the
waist. Black poured himself a small tumbler of Scotch, lifted
his glass to Chant, sipped. Then he went back to his chair,
leaned back, and studied his friend.

John Sinclair had often remarked that ceremony could en-
hance the pleasure of many things, yet Black was still struck
by many of the small things his friend did, such as the ritual

he went through in consuming the tiny amount of saki in his cup. The ex-convict knew that Chant would take as much as fifteen minutes to drink the saki, and during this time he would not wish to speak. Sitting straight in his chair with both feet on the floor, Chant would take tiny sips of the rice wine as he stared straight ahead, his eyes slightly out of focus. The expression on his face would be distant, as though the smell and taste of the saki were evoking memories of . . . Tony Black did not know what.

And then his own memories began to flow.

Black recalled how he had met John Sinclair many years before, at a boot camp in Georgia, where they had become friends; yet now, when he thought about it, he was amazed at how little—virtually nothing—he knew of the other man's life before it had intersected with his own. Indeed, it had not even occurred to him until many years later—when there were no longer bullets flying through the air, and he had only the demons in his mind to contend with, and he had lots of time to reflect in his prison cell—that John Sinclair had never spoken of his background, where he had been or what he had done, before joining the Army at the age of twenty-three.

Black had always assumed that Chant had been born and raised in the United States; now, as he watched the man go through his ritual of drinking saki, he questioned this assumption. Not that it made any difference. The mystery surrounding John Sinclair did not bother Black now any more than it had when they were together in Southeast Asia. The only thing that had mattered there was whether or not a man could be trusted and could fight. John Sinclair had always been trusted by everyone whose opinion was worth anything. And he was the best fighter—with any weapon, from antitank gun to his bare hands and feet—Black had ever seen, before or since. Upon entering the Army, John Sinclair had already been a consummate master of the martial arts, and no one, at least not to Tony Black's knowledge, had ever learned how or where the twenty-three-year-old had acquired his skills.

Memories of fighting . . . of awesome technique pitted

against monstrous brutality; the epic duel between the young
John Sinclair and the maniacal Tommy Wing, the man they
called Hammerhead, a fight which had landed both men in an
Army hospital for weeks. Black considered Tommy Wing, a
man apparently impervious to pain, to be the most dangerous
and terrifying man he had ever met—but he knew there were
many who would think and say the same of the man sitting
across from him, savoring a tiny cup of saki.

Memories . . .

They had trained together, fought together, been promoted
together—at least for a time. Senior officers began to take
notice of, and reward, John Sinclair's fighting and leadership
skills, and there were many who predicted a long and illustrious military career for the young man with the iron-colored
eyes and hair, with his eventually becoming the youngest general in U.S. Army history. They had even been recruited by
the CIA at about the same time, and had become Company
operatives in addition to their Army duties.

Then their careers had gone in different directions. Chant
had been assigned to the CIA's secret war in Laos, his mission
to equip, train, and fight with the Hmong villagers against the
Pathet Lao. Almost two and a half years had gone by, and then
the stories had begun trickling back of the fierce American
who had become a legend to the Hmong, and was the Pathet
Lao's most feared enemy, a man upon whose head they had
placed a great price.

And then had come the devastating rumors of Chant's de-
sertion. The rumors hinted of something terrible that had happened, a dark event that had involved Chant—but no more.
Then even the rumors had stopped when a tight lid of secrecy
had been clamped down and the men had been forbidden ever
to speak of John Sinclair and the story that he had killed six
American servicemen in the process of deserting.

Memories . . . and loss of them.

Eventually, Black had forgotten John Sinclair. Black had
survived combat in Vietnam, then returned to a society that

suddenly seemed alien to him. Emotionally scarred like so many Vietnam veterans, he couldn't seem to keep a job, couldn't function with nightmare memories which even vast amounts of liquor didn't wash away. Eventually he'd turned to crime. Caught and convicted of armed robbery, he had served eleven years in prison before gaining an early release on parole as a model prisoner.

With the help of the Fortune Society, he had found a job and rebuilt his life. When he had been elected President, he had been told by his predecessor that a considerable part of the society's operating budget came from an anonymous donor living somewhere in Europe.

The donor had turned out to be John Sinclair, who had decided to make himself known to an astonished Tony Black. Their friendship had blossomed anew, and since then Black had learned that John Sinclair represented many things to many people: he was either an unspeakably brutal vigilante and terrorist, or a man of unmatched courage and kindness who carried on a global war for justice as a kind of one-man mercenary army. The most amusing—and, Black had often mused, possibly accurate—description of John Sinclair the ex-convict had ever heard had come from an FBI agent who'd called him a "badass Robin Hood who steals from the rich and gives to the poor—after taking a big cut for himself."

For Tony Black, it was enough that John Sinclair was simply his friend.

"Thank you," Chant said, leaning forward and placing the empty china cup on Black's desk. "I enjoyed that very much."

"Another one?"

Chant shook his head. "One is enough."

"Are you here for the holidays?" Black asked carefully, not wishing to seem to pry.

"Perhaps," Chant replied. "Actually, I was in Florida recently for quite a while."

"Business?"

"Paying a visit to some crooked nursing-home operators."

Tony Black smiled. "Sounds like small potatoes for the infamous international criminal and extortionist, John Sinclair."

"It wasn't small potatoes for the old people who were trapped in the home."

"I'm sorry, Chant," Black said quietly. "I was trying to be funny, and I made a bad joke. I didn't mean to be insensitive."

"I know that," Chant said easily. "By the way, you'll be interested to know that Alistair played a key role in putting those guys out of business."

"Alistair!" Black cried, grinning. "How the hell is that feisty old bastard?"

"Still feisty, for sure," Chant replied with a wry smile. "Alistair's a good man, Tony."

"How much does he know by now about the man he's working for?"

Chant shrugged. "He knows enough to know not to talk about what he knows."

Black splashed some more Scotch into his tumbler, but did not drink. "Speaking of criminals," he said in a soft, serious tone as he stared down into the amber-colored liquid, "I heard a rumor a couple of months ago that the state had let Hammerhead out of whatever hospital for the criminally insane they'd been keeping him in." Black paused, looked up at Chant, and shook his head in disgust. "Can you imagine letting that fucking cannibal loose on the streets? I mean, there were a lot of 'fragging' incidents in that war, potheads throwing a fragmentation grenade into the tent of a CO he didn't like; but that fucking Tommy Wing literally chewed his CO to death."

Chant felt the puckered scars on his belly, thighs, and arms slowly begin to throb, burning with a kind of cold fire. "Tommy Wing is here in New York?"

Black lifted the tumbler and drained it off, set it back down on the desk. "I don't know if he's here now—in fact, I don't know for sure that he was ever here. One of the guys who was with us in 'Nam said he saw him coming out of Bloomingdale's, of all places. That was some time ago, maybe a year or more. The guy could have been mistaken."

"Tommy Wing would be hard to mistake for anyone else," Chant said in a low, flat voice.

"That's for sure. Anyway, he's damn well never come in here, even though he'd be eligible for membership."

"Why? He was in a mental hospital, not prison."

"He was behind bars, which is just about the only criterion we use. Which is not to say that I'd be here if he were; there's no way I'd share membership in any organization with Tommy Wing."

Chant smiled thinly, without humor. "Maybe he's all better now."

"Sure he is," Black said with a sharp laugh. "It's more likely the hospital got overcrowded, or he started to spook the shrinks. Shit, I'll never forget that fight between you two. You're the only man who ever defeated Hammerhead."

"I didn't defeat him, Tony. It was a standoff."

"Fighting Hammerhead to a standoff was the same as defeating him. Before you came along, and before the Army threw him in the stockade after he bit out that major's throat, he'd used those big buck teeth of his to cripple a half dozen men. From the stockade he went straight to Matteawan, and I really can't understand why they'd let him out." Black paused, shrugged. "So much for the walk down memory lane. Chant, will you have dinner with me?"

"I counted on it. But first, there's something you can do for me."

"Name it."

"Two days ago, a friend of mine was shot and killed."

"I'm sorry, Chant."

Chant nodded. "He was gunned down on a street in Rome by an American ex-convict."

"The Italian magistrate?"

"Yes. His name was Vito Biaggi."

"I read about it in the papers. He sounded like a good man, Chant."

"He was. His killer's name was Tyrone Good. Alistair said he knew him in prison, and that Good had also been a member of the Fortune Society here in New York. It would have been a few years ago. I thought you might remember him."

Black thought about it, shook his head. "If Alistair says Good was a member, then he was a member. The name just doesn't ring a bell. He may not have been that active, or I simply may have not run into him. We have a lot of members."

"I'm sorry to hear you didn't know him. I was hoping you might be able to tell me something about him."

"The papers said he was just a crazy doing a crazy thing. You think there may be more to it?"

"I don't know, Tony."

Black turned in his chair and glanced at the file cabinet across the room. "We don't really keep records, as such, on our members," he said tentatively. "It's not what we're about. But we do keep a card file for purposes of employment—which kinds of jobs have worked out for certain kinds of people, good sources of employment, that kind of thing. I can rummage around, if you'd like, see if there's anything in there on Tyrone Good."

"I'd appreciate it. While you're at it, I'd also like to know if you have any information on a man named Axle Trent."

"Another one of us?"

"I don't know. He's another American ex-convict who shot down a prominent diplomat in Switzerland a few months ago. Like Good, he didn't seem to have any motive for what he did, no passport that anyone could find, and no reason for being in Europe."

Black rose, walked across the room, opened the top drawer of the file cabinet, and began searching through it. Five minutes later, he apparently found what he was looking for. He grunted, slowly walked back to his desk carrying two sets of papers loosely held together with paper clips.

"Trent was a member, too," Black said as he sat back down in his chair. Behind the thick lenses of his glasses, his eyes glowed with obvious interest. "He's another one I never met."

"I'd like to know what, if anything, the two men might have had in common. Anything at all."

Black nodded, began leafing through both sets of papers. "You're welcome to look at these," he said absently, "but the guy who wrote these up has worse handwriting than mine, and I can probably read it a lot better than you can."

"You go ahead. As I said, what I'm looking for is a common link, if there is any."

Black continued to pore over the papers, alternating his attention between one set and the other. After a few minutes he looked up and shook his head. "About the only thing I can find here that they had in common was that they were both bad news—real losers. They were both longtimers, but one was in San Quentin—that would be the one Alistair knew—and the other in Folsom. They got out about a year apart, came here to New York. One had been in for murder two, and the other on seven counts of rape. Neither one was here for very long, and the society obviously couldn't do much for either one."

"Could they have known each other?"

"Extremely unlikely that they even met. As I said, they got out roughly a year apart, came to New York, and left—or at least dropped out of active membership in the society—after a short time. There's no indication that either ever landed a job, and judging from what's in these records we wouldn't have recommended either one to any of our good employers. Both of them picked up a little cash by agreeing to participate in a research project, and there's nothing on them after that."

"What about the research project, Tony? That sounds like a common link."

Black pushed aside the papers. "A totally predictable one. Show me a long-term ex-convict living in the city, and I'll show you a man who's probably picked up a couple of bucks over at Blake College, which is a small school in Brooklyn. The psychology department at Blake has been running an ongoing project for years, using ex-convicts as test subjects."

"What's the purpose of the research?"

"As I understand it, they want to compare the overall physical health of long-term ex-convicts with the normal population outside. The project's funded by a bunch of insurance companies. I haven't got the slightest idea what they want to find out, but it's a good deal for a lot of our people—gives them a chance to pick up a little extra cash."

"Did you participate in it, Tony?"

The President of the Fortune Society shook his head. "Not eligible. When they say they want long-termers, they mean *serious* long-termers: fifteen years or longer. I didn't make the grade."

"That's the only qualification for participation?"

"The way I understand it, that's it. By now, there must be hundreds of men who've taken part in it. Long-termers are referred by friends, social workers, psychiatrists, whoever."

"Blake College takes all comers?"

"You've got the picture; all comers who've been incarcerated fifteen years or longer."

"You didn't know Good or Trent. Are there any people you do know who've been in the program?"

"Sure. Alistair, for one."

"Besides Alistair."

Black cocked his head to one side, drummed his fingertips on the desktop. "Offhand, I can think of six," he said at last.

"Alistair works for me. Good and Trent ended up killing people in Europe. What's happened to the six men you know?"

"Well, let's see...two are still working steady jobs they've had for some time. Another got laid off last month and is collecting unemployment. If you want to talk to them, I can arrange it."

"Maybe I will. I'll let you know. You said you knew six men who'd been in the program. What happened to the other three?"

"One died in a drowning accident two summers ago. I lost touch with the other two. They dropped out of sight, probably left the city. One, a guy by the name of Ron Press, ended up somewhere in Texas. I happen to know his girlfriend, and she got a letter from him last summer apologizing for leaving in such a hurry and without saying good-bye. From what this woman told me, his letter made it sound like he was in pretty good shape—said he had a job in a pharmaceuticals plant. I never heard anything from him, which doesn't surprise me. We were never what you would call friends, and I never much cared for him; I found him more than a little paranoid, with a hair-trigger temper. Still, if he did finally latch on to a job he can hold, I'm happy for him."

Chant was silent for some time, staring out the window at the streets of Manhattan ablaze with Christmas lights and decorations.

"Chant? You need to know anything else?"

Chant turned his attention from the window, smiled at the other man. "Not now, Tony. Thanks. Why don't you pick us out a good restaurant?"

Black grunted. He was silent for some time, an odd expression on his face, as he studied the half of his friend's face that was not now hidden in shadow in the poorly lighted office.

"God," he said at last in a very low voice, "they must have laid something really heavy on you."

"Who, Tony? What are you talking about?"

"Sorry," Black said, abruptly lowering his gaze. "It's none of my damn business. The talk about Hammerhead triggered memories. I remembered the way things were back in 'Nam, and then hearing about the incredible job you were doing fighting with the Hmong up in Laos. Everyone said you were going to be sitting with the Joint Chiefs one day. Then, the next thing we hear is that you'd deserted. Chant, I hit the first man who said that to me, knocked out a couple of his teeth, and almost got myself court-martialed. I said there was no way John Sinclair would have deserted, unless...I don't know. I'm saying you must have had one hell of a good reason."

"I thought I did," Chant said evenly. "You're my friend, Tony, and I obviously trust you with my life and freedom. Because you're my friend, I tell you that you don't want to know the reason why I walked away from the war. It would do you no good to know, and it's the kind of information that could conceivably get you killed one day if our relationship ever became known. It could also cost you a lot of sleepless nights."

"There was . . . a story that you killed six American servicemen."

"True. They were trying to kill me. No more, Tony."

"You want to do Japanese? Maybe Szechuan? There's a really fine place just up the street."

"Actually, if it's all the same to you, I'd prefer a good American steak house."

"Christ Cella?"

"Perfect."

"The CIA?" Black asked quietly. "Are they the reason you walked away? Are they the people who want you dead?"

Chant laughed easily, rose, and walked to the door. "Come, my friend. Let's go get something to eat."

field of fire and fangs ─────

Chant, by his estimate, was a third of the way through the course—a netherworld of acres of flame, choking smoke, barbed wire, and machine-gun fire raking through the air four feet above the ground at irregular intervals—when the first snake struck. Chant heard the rattle and saw the movement of the serpent's head a split second before it came at him; his hand moved with lightning speed, catching the six-foot-long timber rattlesnake around its thick neck. He smashed its head against a rock, then threw its carcass into a fountain of flame to his right as machine-gun bullets suddenly began to whine through the air over his head. Then the firing stopped, and Chant could hear the shouts of frightened men above the omnipresent crackling of the flames.

Chant thought he knew what had happened: the flames, smoke, barbed wire, and gunfire on this field at an abandoned Army base in upstate New York were there by design, intended to test the men's nerve and courage under conditions of extreme stress; but the rattlesnakes were a deadly surprise.

Montsero had had the incredible bad fortune to lay out the course over a nesting area where untold numbers of the deadly reptiles had been roused from hibernation by the heat of the flames, which meant there was a good possibility that the psychologist was going to lose a number of the increasingly elite group during the course of this particular trial.

At the moment, Chant thought with a wry smile, there weren't too many men on the course left worrying about winning the thousand-dollar bonus that went to the man who finished first; they'd be too busy worrying about the snakes hissing in their faces as machine-gun bullets filled the air over their heads.

He grabbed three more snakes as they slithered toward him and threw them into the fire, clearing the immediate area. When he heard a scream to his left, he sucked in a deep breath, rose from his belly into a crouch, and darted through a cloud of black, acrid smoke, circumvented a wall of flames, heading toward the sound. He found himself in a small area of burned-out ground. In the center of the area was a rangy, short-tempered man Chant knew as Chuck Politan. His face, beneath the dagger tattoos on both cheeks, was ashen as he stared, frozen with panic, at the huge rattlesnake coiled to strike in front of him. He cradled his tattooed right forearm in his left hand, and even from yards away Chant could see the crimson fang marks in the black ink of the arm. Politan saw Chant, and his eyes went wide with both horror and appeal. He opened his mouth to speak, but no sound came out.

"Be still!" Chant shouted in order to be heard over the rattle of gunfire and roar of the flames.

"I'm going to die!" the tattooed man screamed.

"Not if you do as I say! Lie still!"

Chant slowly crawled forward in an easy, flowing motion toward the man and the snake. The rattler finally struck at Politan, but Chant struck even faster, his hand darting out and closing around the snake's neck as streams of cloudy venom squirted from the extended hypodermic fangs, splashing over the faces of both men. In a single, fluid motion,

Chant rolled over on his back and hurled the snake away.

"Jesus Christ!" *Politan shouted, shaking his head in relief, shock, and disbelief. "Alter, you are one fast son-of-a-bitch! I never even saw your hand move!"*

"Be very still," *Chant said calmly.* "Montsero has a medical kit with antivenom serum. There's venom in your system right now, but we have time." *Chant removed his belt, tightened it around the man's right forearm, above the fang marks.* "You won't die if you can control your panic. Try to relax and breathe as deeply as you can without choking on the smoke. Panic just flushes the poison through your system faster."

"How the hell are we going to get out of here?! I don't know which way to go!"

"I do."

"But we're surrounded by fire! We'll burn to death!"

"Be still, Politan, or you're going to shout yourself to death. I said I'd get you out."

The tattooed man stared at Chant, blinked, then visibly relaxed as Chant gripped his wrist and began leading him to the opposite side of the burned-out area. "You know, Alter, damned if I don't believe you really can get me out of here in time."

And Chant did.

Outside the perimeter of the flames, while Politan was being treated by one of Montsero's assistants, Chant abruptly turned away from the plain of fire, and as he did so caught a glint of sunlight off glass or metal midway up the side of a mountain in the distance.

The Watcher, Chant thought. He had been right.

CHAPTER THREE _____

"Chant!"

Chant wrapped his arms around the slight, gray-haired woman who rushed out onto the porch of her East Side brownstone to greet him. He bent down and kissed Martha Greenblatt, then hurried her back through the door. "Come on, love," he said, closing the door on a savage gust of wind. "You're going to catch pneumonia running around in the cold like that with no coat on."

"Not likely," Martha Greenblatt said as she took Chant's sheepskin coat and hung it up in a hall closet. "*Lord,* it's good to see you. Harry will be so sorry he missed you." The woman paused, reached out, and gently stroked Chant's massive chest. "When I don't see or hear from you in months, I'm always so afraid you're either dead or in prison, and I'll never even know about it."

"If I'm ever on my way to prison, you can be sure you'll hear about it. What would be the sense of having the best lawyer in the world as a friend and not using her when you need her?"

The woman laughed lightly as she took Chant's arm and led him into a living room beautifully furnished with fine Persian carpets and French antiques. "Not so good a lawyer anymore, Chant. Just an old courtroom brawler who does a little *pro bono* work here and there to keep the gray matter from drying up."

"You always did *pro bono* work, my dear, for anyone who needed it."

Martha Greenblatt eased Chant down onto a couch beneath a Monet in a gold frame, sat down beside him, and took his hand. "I wouldn't be doing any kind of work if you hadn't fished me out of the Hudson ten years ago."

"I was lucky to be in the right place at the right time. I'd been tracking that neo-Nazi client of yours for three months. You should have been—should be—more careful about the people you choose to represent."

"Now, Chant," the woman said, clucking her tongue. "Who better than John Sinclair would know that guilt or innocence has nothing to do with the practice of law?" She paused, squeezed his hand. "I was so happy when you called. Can you stay for a few hours?"

"Overnight, if you're willing to put me up."

"Good! Harry's due back from Spain tomorrow, and he'll be delighted to see you." Martha Greenblatt clapped her hands with delight, like a child, and her pale green eyes gleamed with pleasure. "I'm going to prepare a fine dinner, but first we'll have tea! You can stand over my shoulder to make certain I get that ceremony you taught me right."

"That would be very nice. But if we're going to enjoy a tea ceremony, then I'll get the business part of my visit out of the way first."

"What can I do for you, Chant?" Martha Greenblatt asked, sitting up straight and folding her hands in her lap. Suddenly the retired attorney, who had been one of the country's foremost criminal trial lawyers as well as a recognized authority on constitutional law, was all business.

"Give me some information, if you can. Are you familiar with the research project involving ex-convicts over at Blake College?"

"Yes," the woman replied easily, curiosity evident in her voice. "Why?"

"You think it's legitimate?"

"Meaning?"

"I'm not sure what I mean. I'd just like to know what you think."

"What's not to be legitimate? It's a long-range thing, been going on for years. It's an easy way for ex-convicts who qualify to pick up a few dollars by sitting around for a couple of hours filling out questionnaires."

"Is that what they do?"

"So I'm told."

"I intend to find out for myself. I need to know what the most common procedures are for referral or application. I don't want anything about me to seem unusual."

"That may not be so easy, Chant. You can't just go over there, knock on the door and introduce yourself as an ex-convict. They only use long-termers, people who've been locked up fifteen years or longer, and I'm sure they must check with the prison you supposedly came out of."

"I've already done some preliminary work. I'm going to assume the identity of a man by the name of Neil Alter."

"Is there a real Neil Alter?"

Chant nodded. "He just got out of prison after serving twenty years for a murder, which, the authorities finally discovered, he didn't commit. From what I understand, the people at Blake College don't care whether you're guilty or innocent, only that you've served time."

"That's right. But why Neil Alter?"

"According to the newspapers I researched, he's about my size, and I should be able to construct a fairly simple disguise to resemble his other physical characteristics. He comes from the Everglades section of Florida, which means the chances of his showing up in New York City are minimal. Naturally, I'll have appropriate identity papers."

Martha Greenblatt shrugged her shoulders. "In that case, there's no problem. You finish putting yourself together as Neil Alter, and I'll pick up the phone and have you in the project in five minutes."

Chant shook his head.

"Why not, Chant? It would be so simple."

"Martha, this may turn out to be a waste of my time. Then again, it may not. I don't know what I'm going to find over there. If something does happen, I don't want anyone to be able to connect you with Neil Alter."

"Now you're being silly. You wouldn't be the first person I've sent over there."

"I'd be the first phony. And even if I were willing to risk having you linked with me, which I'm not, I wouldn't want you to refer me. You're too illustrious a celebrity, and your name might attract attention. As long as I've set things up properly, why can't I just go over and apply?"

"You could. But you said that you didn't want anything about you to seem unusual. Your home is in Florida, and you just got out of prison. What are you going to tell them when they ask what you're doing in New York? Of course, you'll come up with a good reason—but it will certainly seem like an *unusual* reason. Don't you think so?"

Chant gave a slight nod of his head. "Your point is well taken, Martha. See why I came to you?"

"What you need is referral by a social worker. That way, the people at Blake will figure all the tough questions have been asked and you've already been screened. They might not even check your prison record."

Chant smiled, kissed his friend on the cheek. "Thank you, Martha; you're a wonder. Tomorrow, after saying hello to Harry, I move down to the Bowery."

Martha Greenblatt playfully pushed Chant away, then made

a not-so-playful gesture of disdain with her hand. "Talk about wasting time! If you try to get next to a social worker by going the Bowery bum and Salvation Army route, it'll take you two months just to go to interviews and fill out welfare forms. Believe me; I know what I'm talking about. If you won't let me refer you directly to the project over at Blake, at least let me refer you to a social worker."

Chant smiled. "And what would I tell the social worker when he or she starts asking the tough questions?"

"Are you kidding me? I said the people at Blake might *assume* they'd been asked, not that they actually had been. Do you have any idea of the size of the *caseload* for the average social worker in New York City?! I'm serious, Chant."

"I don't think so, Martha. There'd still be a link."

"But not the same kind of link. It's not a big deal, Chant. Really. I would consider it a great privilege to help you. Will you tell me why you want to go over there?"

Again, Chant smiled, "Nope."

"You listen to me, John Sinclair. With all the *pro bono* work I do, I deal with social agencies all the time. There are a dozen different ways I could have met you, and there would be nothing suspicious about my referring Neil Alter to one of them. In fact, I already know what I'd like to do; I'll refer you to a woman by the name of Jan Rawlings. She's a pretty young thing, just getting started in the social work business and getting a bitter taste of just how rough New York City can be if you're down and out. I like her, even if she is—or maybe *because* she is—a hopeless idealist. I'm sure meeting you will be good for her, no matter who she thinks you are."

Chant, still smiling, said nothing.

"Are you thinking about it?" Martha Greenblatt asked.

"Nope."

"There'd be no danger to Jan, if that's what you're worried about. Even if something did happen and you were found out, there's no way on God's earth anyone would hold a poor, overworked caseworker responsible for not spotting a ringer. When will you be ready to be Neil Alter?"

"I'm not going to tell you, madam."

"Will you think about it?"

"Nope."

Suddenly the laughter was gone from Martha Greenblatt's voice and eyes. "Yes, you will," she said very seriously. "You make a virtual fetish out of working alone, because you're so afraid of an innocent person being hurt because of you. Well, there's no way anyone—except you, of course, but that's always the case—can be hurt by the procedure I'm recommending. I didn't earn my reputation as a pretty good trial lawyer by being unpersuasive. You'll think about it, then realize that it's pointless to waste time freezing on the sidewalk and getting chewed on by rats when it's possible—without risk to anyone but yourself—to get right on with the business that brought you here." The woman paused, broke into a grin. "Any more business?"

"Nope."

"Good!" Martha's eyes now sparkled with delight. "Then you'll please come and supervise my preparation of the tea. I have all the things you bought for me laid out—something I did right after I hung up. The ceremony is lovely, but I'm sure I've forgotten everything you taught me."

"I doubt it," Chant said dryly as he rose from the couch, offered his arm, and let the woman lead him toward the dining room. "You never forget anything, Martha."

CHAPTER FOUR ─────────

MUSIC FROM A Salvation Army band wafted up from the street seventeen stories below, penetrated the Thermopane window and grated against Jan Rawling's senses. The trombone was at least half a pitch flat, Jan thought, and she wondered if the player knew, or cared. In the three years since she'd graduated from college and come to New York City, Jan had come to hate the Christmas season. She hated having to buy gifts, but knew that she had to in order to avoid embarrassment when she received them; she hated signing and addressing the five dozen or so cards she mailed out each year, received no pleasure from the five dozen or so she got in return. She longed to join a Skip Christmas Club.

Like every year at this time, she was very depressed.

Jan hated Christmas parties, but always felt compelled to attend the annual office party for fear that she would offend her co-workers if she didn't. For the same reason, she always felt compelled to accept a drink, but even one usually proved to be too much, leaving her feeling flushed and nauseous. The storage-turned-conference room where the party was being held was overheated, and Jan felt decidedly uncomfortable.

She jumped when she felt the back of someone's hand deliberately brush across her buttocks. She spun around and found herself staring down at Roger Wheeler, a short cipher of a man with fleece on his face that was meant to pass as a beard. Wheeler was a recent graduate who parted his hair in the middle, wore tweed jackets with leather patches on the sleeves, affected to smoke a pipe, and played with hand-held electronic games on his coffee breaks and lunch hours. His face was usually a blank, except for his eyes, which stared at any woman with naked longing.

"I've got a message for you, babe," Wheeler said, a leer in his voice and his eyes fixed on Jan's large breasts.

Most of all she hated sex, Jan thought as she glared at Wheeler. After three boyfriends, including one live-in lover, she'd decided that she would never experience the pleasure other women seemed to find in the act. To her, sex meant only bad smells and ugly slapping sounds, pain and blood and acute embarrassment; it meant grunting men groping her, sucking her breasts as if they were infants, sweating on her, staining her sheets.

Sex and Christmas, Jan thought, were two things she could definitely do without.

"You're a little jumpy tonight," Wheeler continued in his nasal, slightly whining voice. "What you need is another drink or two. Why don't you and I go someplace where it's quiet and we can mellow out?"

"I wouldn't get into an elevator with you, Roger," Jan replied in a voice quivering with anger. She instantly made a vow that the next time Roger Wheeler touched her breasts, legs, or buttocks she would, without hesitation, slam her fist into his nose. "Now, what did you come to say?"

Wheeler, whose gaze had not left Jan's breasts, glanced up, shrugged. "There's a guy downstairs looking for you. I showed him which desk was yours."

"Client?"

"I assume so."

"Roger, it's Christmas Eve!"

"So what?" Wheeler replied, flashing a vaguely malicious smile. "You've been doing nothing for the past half hour but stand and stare out the window, so I figured you wouldn't mind helping some poor, unfortunate wretch looking for some"—Wheeler dropped his gaze to Jan's breasts again—"milk of human kindness."

"I owe you one, Roger," Jan said tightly as she stepped around the short man and headed for the stairs.

She was depressed enough, Jan thought as she descended the narrow stairway to the large, common office area on the floor below. Tonight, at least, she simply could not deal with any more of the endless, reeking river of social waste that constantly flowed into this building.

She stepped into the room, then came to an abrupt halt when she saw the man sitting in the straight-backed chair in front of her desk. Clean-shaven, his nose and cheeks were still red from the bitter cold outside. He was inexpensively but warmly dressed in a down jacket, jeans, and sneakers. As had happened the first time she had seen him, on an emergency referral from Martha Greenblatt, Jan felt a curious pulling sensation in the pit of her stomach when he turned in his chair and looked at her, and she unconsciously reached up with both hands to straighten her long, blond hair. When she had first met with him a week before, the tall, dark-haired and dark-eyed man had been courteous but aloof, politely but firmly refusing her offer to provide him with vocational and social counseling; Jan found she was happy he had decided to come back.

"Hello," Chant said, rising. His smile was so warm and sincere that it made Jan suddenly realize how insincere were most of the smiles she encountered in her daily life. "I'd like your help now, if you can give it. I'm still not in the market for counseling, but I'd appreciate it very much if you could simply help me find a job. It's pretty rough out there, rougher than I thought it would be when I walked out of here last week, and it won't be long before I run out of the little money I've managed to save."

Jan's mouth felt dry, and she licked her lips. It astounded her how, even when standing still, this man with the massive shoulders somehow projected a lithe, easy grace of movement. "Mr. Alter, it's Christmas Eve," she said quietly.

"Christmas doesn't mean much to me. I was in the neighborhood, and I figured it was as easy to come up as to call. Now I see that I've disturbed you. I'm sorry."

"Wait, Mr. Alter," Jan said as Chant turned and headed for the door.

Chant turned in the doorway and studied the strikingly beautiful—and obviously sad—young woman with the long, silky blond hair and soulful, dark brown eyes. Throughout the course of an hour-long interview, Jan Rawlings had never mentioned the possibility of his entering the research project at Blake College, and it had occurred to him that she might not even know about it. Now he considered telling her outright that he had heard about it, then asking if she would refer him. Finally, he decided against that approach. There was always the possibility that the school was closed down for the holidays, and he thought it better not to press.

"There's no need for you to give me any more of your time, Miss Rawlings," Chant said easily. "I've said what I came to tell you. I haven't been able to get a phone installed yet, but I'll call you after New Year's—or sooner, if it's convenient. I was just hoping you might know someone who'd give me work. I'm going to run into a cash problem very soon."

"Please, Mr. Alter," Jan said, walking to her desk. "Come back and sit down."

Chant hesitated, then walked back across the office. He remained standing, his hands resting on the back of the straight-backed chair.

"I apologize, Mr. Alter," Jan continued as she eased herself down into her own chair. "I didn't mean to be rude."

"You weren't rude; I've been rude. I dropped in on you

unannounced, and I've made you leave your party."

"Do I smell of liquor?" Jan asked anxiously.

"No. I can hear the voices and laughter upstairs."

"Oh. Well, we can talk. Really; I wasn't enjoying myself, anyway. I guess Christmas doesn't mean that much to me, either."

Chant searched the woman's face. "Why do you say that?" he asked quietly.

"Because it's true." Jan tried to smile, but the effort made her face ache.

"I'd say Christmas upsets you," Chant said in the same soft, even voice.

Jan found herself staring back into the man's eyes, momentarily transfixed. Finally, she slowly nodded her head.

"Then Christmas does mean something to you," Chant continued matter-of-factly. "It means sadness."

"Yes," Jan replied in a voice that was barely above a whisper. "I guess you're right."

"I hope I haven't offended you."

"You haven't, Mr. Alter." Jan felt giddy, but not from liquor. Something about Neil Alter had an unsettling effect on her, and she dropped her gaze to her desktop. "You've been looking for work, I take it."

"Yes, but I haven't been able to find anyone who'll hire me with my record. I thought I could."

"But you've been pardoned."

"It doesn't make any difference. All that seems to matter when I fill out applications is that I've spent twenty years in prison."

Jan looked up, nodded. "Frankly, it doesn't surprise me; New York City can be a very cold and callous place. Have you spoken to Mrs. Greenblatt about your problem?"

"Mrs. Greenblatt isn't in the job-getting business; I understood that you were."

"Not exactly. As I told you at our last meeting, we do vocational testing and counseling. Then we usually refer our clients to the state employment office for help in actual job placement. If you need money right away, I can arrange for emergency financial assistance."

"I don't want charity, Miss Rawlings," Chant said evenly, "I want work. I misunderstood your offer. I've come to the wrong place."

"No," Jan said quickly, suddenly realizing that she did not want the man to leave. "You didn't misunderstand. It's just that—"

"Miss Rawlings, I'm willing to do any kind of work. I mean that literally. You don't have to give me aptitude tests, because I'm not looking for a career. All I want is work, no matter how menial. I'll be quite happy washing dishes, cleaning bathrooms, or digging holes in the ground. What I do doesn't concern me in the least. In fact, I enjoy physical labor. If you choose to recommend me to someone, I promise that you won't be embarrassed. An employer will find me a punctual and steady worker. I work hard, I don't steal, and I don't often get sick."

"I believe you, Mr. Alter, " Jan said quietly. "I'll see what I can do."

"Thank you."

"The problem is, this just isn't a good time. The department stores will be laying off most of the part-time staff they hired for the seasonal rush; to be blunt, I don't think I can find you a job in a store, anyway. It's the slow season for most kinds of labor. Not much will be happening until after the holidays."

"I understand. If I haven't found a job on my own by then, I'll give you a call after New Year's."

"Just a minute, Mr. Alter," Jan said as she remembered the form letter she had received in the mail a week before. "There just may be something . . ." She quickly searched through the center drawer in her desk until she finally found the letter stuck between two client folders. She pulled out the letter and passed it across the desk to Chant. "You can keep this; look it over and see if it interests you. We get a letter from these people every three or four months. What it boils down to is a call for volunteers who were long-term convicts to participate in some kind of experiment they're running in the psychology department at Blake College, in Brooklyn. All the men in the project must have spent at least fifteen years in prison. It doesn't say anything about being guilty of what they put you away for, so I don't see why you wouldn't qualify. You're the first ex-inmate I've ever worked with, so I really can't tell you much about it—in fact, I didn't even think of it until just now. They pay participants, although probably not much. If they accept you into the program, at least you can pick up some spending money for a few hours of your time; that could be some help until we can find you something more permanent. In the meantime, I'll ask around."

"Thank you," Chant said as he casually folded the letter and put it into the back pocket of his jeans. "I'll give it some thought."

"And you'll call me a week or so after New Year's? I may have a line on something for you by then."

"Thank you."

Jan watched the big man with the gentle voice and manner head toward the door. She still did not want him to go—or she wanted to leave with him, talk some more. She wanted to explore the strange feelings he excited in her—perhaps discover why she had the distinct impression that Martha Greenblatt knew this man much better than the lawyer had indicated. She wanted to ask Neil Alter to stay just a while longer, but she could not seem to make the words come out of her mouth.

"I want to wish you a Merry Christmas," Chant said as he paused in the doorway and turned back to the woman. "I mean that most sincerely."

"I know you do," Jan said in a small voice. She felt short of breath.

"Either you should make your Christmas happy, or you should make it absolutely nothing at all. To allow it to be a source of unhappiness is to indulge yourself in a negative fashion. You don't have to feel the way you do."

Jan licked her dry lips, nodded slightly. "Mr. Alter, are you . . . uh, are you staying with anyone for the holidays?"

"No," Chant replied evenly. "I came to New York because I thought a big city would afford me the best chance for starting a new life, but I don't have any friends here."

Starting a new life, Jan thought, the words causing an ache in her mind as long moments passed in awkward silence. She knew that now was the time to speak; as lonely as she was, she imagined that Neil Alter was even lonelier—this was his first Christmas outside prison walls in twenty years, and he had no one to share it with. She had no one she wished to share it with—except, perhaps, him. She knew she should reach out . . .

And then the moment was gone.

"Well, Merry Christmas to you," Jan said with a forced gaiety that was an absolute contradiction of the emptiness she felt inside.

She watched him smile again—the smile that was so warm and that made her feel, for the moment, that she was the object of his undivided attention and affection. And then he was gone.

Jan sat in the empty office for some time, staring out the open door into the dimly lighted hallway. Then, for no reason at all that she could think of, she began to cry.

the pit ————————————————

"We've been here ten days now, and this will be the last of these field trials before we return to New York for a few more laboratory tests." Montsero paused, adjusted his glasses, then casually waved the fistful of bills he held in his right hand toward a pit, approximately eight feet deep and ten feet square, that had been dug in the frozen ground. "There'll be a five-thousand-dollar bonus to the last man on his feet in that hole. Anyone who wants to go for the five grand just climbs down in there and defends himself, in any way he chooses, against anyone else who climbs down there with the same idea. Simple. Think of it as a game we'll call 'king of the pit.' All right, go."

Chant slipped out of his parka, removed his boots and socks. He leaped nimbly down into the pit, then turned with his hands at his sides to wait for the other combatants.

The other eleven men slowly fanned out around the edges of the pit.

Chant assumed that the others would band together and all

43

come after him first before trying to decide the issue among themselves. He decided, if that happened, to—for the first time—fully extend himself and his skills as much as was necessary to emerge as the winner in order to see what effect, if any, it would have on what Montsero did with him next.

But nobody jumped down into the pit to challenge him. Over the ten days they had been on the abandoned military preserve, the others had come to appreciate Chant's awesome mental and physical strength, not only in the run and on the field of flame, but in dozens of other tests of skill, strength, intelligence, and endurance; now they had no desire to face him in hand-to-hand combat—not as individuals, nor even as a group.

Tank Olsen was the first to turn and walk away from the pit, as Chant had expected he would. Chuck Politan, absently rubbing his right forearm, was the second to disappear from Chant's field of vision. When all of the men except for Montsero had walked away from the edge, Chant casually climbed up out of the pit, put his parka, boots, and socks back on.

"It looks like you've made quite an impression around here, Alter," Montsero said in a flat voice as he held out the money to Chant.

Behind the man in the reflecting aviator glasses, Chant again saw sunlight glint off binoculars or a rifle high up on a mountain in the distance. The Watcher again, Chant thought, and he was glad he had not been forced to display the full range of his fighting skills.

If, after all of the other men had refused to fight him, that any longer made any difference.

CHAPTER FIVE _____

CHANT HAD RISEN at dawn, emptied the roach traps he'd set, scoured the bathroom, then swept the small studio apartment with a stiff-bristled broom. He'd showered, and was now in the process of shaving. Tea, which he would take with his simple breakfast of bread and cheese, was brewing on his hot plate.

He reacted to the knock on his door with a slight raising of his eyebrows, then quickly put in his contact lenses and donned his dark wig. He could think of no one who would come to see him, and it was an unlikely hour for the legions of burglars who hunted in the neighborhood to be checking apartments to see which were empty.

"Come in," Chant said after the second knock, and deliberately continued his shaving in the small sink by the door as a man in a heavy tweed overcoat and black wool scarf stepped into the room.

Chant glanced over at the man, who unceremoniously unbuttoned his coat and stood waiting in silence. About six feet tall, the man was whippet-thin, with pale brown hair and eyes. An angular, rodentlike face was accentuated by a wispy mustache. There was an antiseptic smell about him, like strong mouthwash or scalp medication.

Chant finished shaving, splashed his face, dried off with a rough, frayed towel. "Who are you?" he asked as he began putting on a shirt he'd hung from a nail driven in the wall.

"My name's Insolers, Mr. Alter," the man said in a high-pitched, reedy voice. "I'm with the Central Intelligence Agency."

The muscles in Chant's stomach fluttered and he felt a slight chill at the base of his spine at the mention of the organization that had been relentlessly hunting him for so many years, but he displayed no reaction as he finished buttoning his shirt. No CIA field operative—if that's what this man really was—would know *why* top executives wanted John Sinclair dead, Chant thought, but his visitor would most certainly experience a little chill of his own if he knew who he was really talking to.

"What do you want?"

"Just a few minutes of your time, Mr. Alter. That's all it will take to find out if we can do business."

There were no chairs in the room, and Chant nodded toward the narrow, swaybacked bed. "Sit, if you'd like."

The man shook his head.

"What business could the CIA possibly have with me?" Chant asked in an even tone, suppressing a smile.

"We know that you've been accepted into Professor Montsero's latest experimental group of ex-convicts. That makes you potentially very valuable to us, Mr. Alter."

"Why?"

"We think you can be trusted. You were wrongfully convicted. That makes you an innocent man, an honest man, chosen to participate in a project with a crew of perverts, murderers, thieves, rapists—and worse. Losers, every single one of Montsero's subjects. Except you. We'd like you to be our eyes and ears in your group. You mind if I smoke?"

Chant stepped into the tiny alcove where he kept his hot plate and a few dishes. He brought a saucer back to Insolers, who had removed his overcoat and sat down on the edge of the bed. Insolers wore a well-tailored suit that matched his eyes, and highly polished boots of fine leather. Chant handed Insolers the saucer. The man lit a Benson & Hedges, dropped the match into the saucer. There was an air of confidence and unhurried appraisal about Insolers, Chant thought as he met the man's steady gaze through a thin haze of smoke. The man knew how to wait, and was probably good at his job—whatever that job might be.

"You have identification?" Chant asked quietly.

The man withdrew a thin leather wallet from his inside coat pocket and handed it to Chant, who flipped it open and examined the laminated, embossed card inside. The real Neil Alter wouldn't know an authentic CIA credential from a parking ticket, but Chant certainly did. The one Insolers carried looked genuine.

"You mind if I check this out?" Chant asked, curious as to what the other man's reaction would be.

Insolers dragged on his cigarette, blew a smoke ring. He seemed almost bored. "Be my guest. The last seven digits of that humongous number on the bottom of the card are an eight-hundred telephone number direct to Langley. Go ahead and call it."

"I don't have a telephone. Why should a spy carry an identification card?"

"So that a man like yourself will give some weight to what I say. I'm not a spy like you see in the movies, Mr. Alter. I don't shoot people, I don't arrange for the overthrow of unfriendly governments, and I don't go skulking around Russian missile sites or Washington apartment complexes. I'm just a domestic errand boy whose biggest concern is staying out of the way of FBI people who zealously guard what they consider to be their turf."

It was probably true, Chant thought as he closed the wallet and handed it back to the man. "How did you find out about me?"

"Let's just say that we have a friend on Blake's clerical staff who provides us with access to all the applications for Montsero's research project."

"You say you want me to be your eyes and ears. What is it that you want me to look and listen for?"

"I don't want to tell you that," Insolers replied matter-of-factly. "It could make you self-conscious, and that could be dangerous for you. We don't want you to do anything unusual; just take part, watch, and listen. I'll drop around from time to time, or leave word where and when we can meet. Then you'll report to me on what goes on. How about it, Mr. Alter? Will you cooperate?"

"I'll give it some thought."

"Look, I imagine you're pretty bitter about what happened to you. Also, judging from the looks of this place, things are pretty rough for you right now. I can understand you being goddam pissed, and maybe you feel you don't owe this country—"

"How I feel about this country will have nothing to do with my decision, Insolers. I don't blame the government, or any person, for what happened to me, and I don't feel bitter. I don't have time or energy to waste on recriminations or regrets."

"What's the problem, then? Did I scare you when I said it might be dangerous if we told you what we were looking for?"

Chant said nothing.

The rodent-faced man grimaced and clucked his tongue. "You're kind of putting me on a spot, Mr. Alter. The first session is scheduled for this afternoon."

"So? Why am I putting you on a spot? I'll be going to the session anyway. By the time you contact me again, I'll have made my decision as to whether or not I have anything to say to you."

"Yeah, but there's information I could give you if I knew you were going to cooperate."

"Do what you want."

Insolers sighed heavily. He ground out his cigarette in the saucer, immediately lit another. "All right," he said after a long pause. "I'm going to give it to you. I'm not sure it will do any good, but it might. To be perfectly frank with you, we haven't quite totally figured out this angle yet."

"Do you expect me to express curiosity, Insolers? All right; I'm curious.

"You have a peculiar way of saying what's on your mind, Mr. Alter."

"So do you," Chant replied evenly. "You come to me waving what you claim is a CIA identity card and asking me to act as an informer on a group of men I've never met—but you won't tell me what I'm supposed to be looking for, or why. For all I know, that card—and you—could be phony. I'm an ex-convict, with no real way of checking you out. Now you're trying to pressure me. I was told two days ago that I'd been accepted into the group. Why did you wait until the day of the first session to contact me?"

Insolers shrugged. "It took us a little time to put things together."

"That tells me nothing. I've been in another world for twenty years, Insolers. You'd best believe that I'm going to ease my way back into this one with great care and caution. In the world I just came from, informing—for whatever reason —is definitely not a good idea."

Insolers narrowed his eyes, slowly nodded. "All right," he said after a pause. "All the talk in the world isn't going to do us any good unless you last and keep making the cuts."

"Keep making the cuts?"

"The experiments are conducted in stages, with the original group growing smaller at each step. There's some kind of elimination process continually going on, and we don't completely understand it because the men chosen to continue are sworn to absolute secrecy about why they were chosen—assuming they know, which is a big assumption—and what they do at each step along the way. Naturally, we'd like to see you get through to the final stage so that we can get the big picture of just what Montsero's so-called research project is really all about. I can't guarantee that you're going to make it that far, no matter what you do. There seem to be a number of criteria applied to the people chosen to continue on, and we don't know what they are. But the first critical step is the multiple-choice tests you'll be taking this afternoon. God knows what they're trying to figure out, but I can tell you this: on every sixth question you should check the fourth box, no matter how ridiculous that answer might seem to you. I told you there's no guarantee, but we have good reason to believe doing that will go a long way toward getting you passed on to the next stage."

"You don't know the purpose of the tests, but you know which boxes I have to check in order to pass them?"

"The intelligence community works in mysterious ways, Mr. Alter," Insolers replied as he stubbed out his cigarette. He rose and put on his overcoat, shrugging it over his thin frame. "Remember: the fourth box on every sixth question."

Chant remained where he was as Insolers left the room, closing the door quietly behind him. The medicinal smell remained, pungent and unpleasant.

There was always the possibility that he had made a mistake and betrayed his presence in New York, Chant thought as he pondered the meaning of Insolers's visit. Both the CIA and FBI would be certain that he was in the United States; the operation against the Johnson brothers in Florida had his mark all over it—precisely as he had intended. There was also the possibility that Alistair had blundered, been captured and drugged or tortured into revealing where he had gone, and why. Insolers's visit could be the CIA's way of playing a cat-and-mouse game with his mind before killing him.

But Chant didn't think so. The CIA didn't work that way; if the agency had had any indication that the man calling himself Neil Alter was really John Sinclair, Chant was certain he'd be dead. Which meant that Duane Insolers, with his apparently authentic CIA credentials, really was interested in Neil Alter and the Blake College research project on ex-convicts.

The situation offered any number of interesting possibilities, Chant thought with a thin smile, as he dismissed Insolers from his mind.

CHAPTER SIX ———————————

BLAKE COLLEGE TURNED out to be easily accessible by subway and bus. Following the directions he had been given, Chant went to the basement of the largest building, in the center of the campus. He found himself in a large, brightly lit lecture hall with close to fifty other men.

Chant leaned back in his chair and stared at the ceiling, affecting boredom but in fact using his highly developed peripheral vision to observe the others. The room was eerily silent, except for the nervous shuffling of feet and an occasional, muffled cough. It confirmed for Chant what Martha had told him in the course of his "briefing" for his role, that ex-convicts on the outside tended to be notoriously shy in the presence of strangers, even if those strangers were ex-convicts like themselves. Most of the men sat very straight in the student desks, feet flat on the floor and arms folded across their chests. Only one other man besides Chant had removed his coat, although the room was warm. The men appeared to range in age from their late thirties to a few well past sixty, with a relatively even mix of whites, blacks, and Hispanics. A lone Oriental sat like a paranoid sentry near the door, as if ready to bolt if he saw or heard something he did not like.

"You don't look like no long-termer to me, and I've got a pretty good eye for things."

Chant turned and looked at the man sitting next to him, who had spoken. The man was the same height as Chant but perhaps seventy pounds heavier, most of it thick and knotted muscle—a man, Chant thought, who had probably lifted weights in the prison yard year after year until he was now too musclebound to do anything with his strength but lift more weights. His head was shaved, and he wore a tiny silver earring in the lobe of his right ear. Both ears were cauliflowered, his nose had apparently been broken many times, and scar tissue around both eyes made it appear as if he were wearing an ivory-colored mask. He was a stupid man with heart, Chant thought, a man who liked to fight, but—unless his face was a secret weapon—not much of a fighter.

"You certainly look like one," Chant replied with a faint smile.

The big man thought about it, then grinned and let out a whoop of laughter that startled half the other men in the room. "Yeah, I guess I do, don't I?"

Chant broadened his own smile. "A real meat-eater, huh?"

"Yeah." The hint of suspicion that had been flickering in the man's eyes was replaced by pride at what he took as a compliment. "You look like you done a lot of easy time."

"A lot of time," Chant said evenly, "none of it easy. Only bankers and politicians do easy time. My only interest in banks was wanting to rob one; I didn't like the only politician I ever met, so I removed his teeth for him."

"You talk good. You been to college or something?"

"Jailhouse University. Started when I was eighteen, studied for twenty years."

"Where?"

"Q," Chant said, hoping the man he was talking to hadn't spent time in San Quentin. "How about you?"

"Attica." The man flexed his right arm, rubbed the shoulder. "Took a rat-trooper bullet right through here during the riots. You can see it's good as new, though. It takes a hell of a lot more than one bullet to put the Tank away. What'd they get you for?"

"Murder," Chant replied, and winked. "Naturally, I didn't do it."

The man whooped again. "They got me for armed robbery and assault. I didn't do none of them things, either. Hey, listen, how about you and me being kind of like, you know, buddies? Maybe we can help each other out during this thing. I never even been *close* to any kind of college, what's more sat in one, and I'm kind of nervous."

"Why not?" Chant extended his hand. "I'm Neil Alter. You, I take it, are Tank?"

"Yeah." The man engulfed Chant's hand in an equally large hand that showed unmistakable signs of arthritis from too many broken bones and dislocated knuckles. "So we'll help each other out if we need it, right?"

"Sure."

"Hey, it looks like the boss man's here."

Precisely at four o'clock a man in a charcoal-gray suit entered the lecture hall. He was short and burly, with feet that seemed too small for the rest of his body. His hair was sandy, streaked with gray, razor-cut. He wore tinted, reflecting aviator glasses, and moved with an air of almost arrogant confidence. Flanking him, carrying bundles of papers, were two extremely attractive student assistants, a boy and a girl, who immediately elicited a chorus of catcalls and sexual remarks from the group. Both students flushed deeply, stopped, and looked down at the floor while the man stepped behind a lectern that had been placed on a slightly elevated platform at the front of the hall. Chant put his age at around fifty.

"I'm Jack Montsero," the man announced in a voice so soft that the group of ex-convicts had to strain in order to hear him. "I'm a shrink. I'm here because I want to find out a few things about you people, and you're here for the money. When we're finished this afternoon, each of you will get a hundred bucks. It'll be in cash, so you don't have to worry about cashing a check."

A low murmur rose from the group. "Hey!" a deep voice called from one of the upper tiers of seats in the back. Chant turned, saw a man with tattoos on his cheeks and hands slouched in his desk with his feet up on the chair in front of him. "You got that much cash on you? How do you know one of us ain't gonna rip you off?"

"What's your name, pal?"

"Chuck Politan, pal. I rob people."

Montsero stepped out from behind the lectern, hunched his broad shoulders, and hooked his thumbs in his belt. "Listen, Politan and the rest of you motherfuckers," he growled in what Chant considered to be a fairly good impression of James Cagney, "there's safety in numbers. If one of you rips me off, it means the rest of you don't get shit. I like those odds. And while we're on the subject of pay, motherfuckers, I want your minds on what I'm saying, and not on what you'd like to do with these two young innocents I've brought along with me."

The impression and the words had the desired effect, and the lecture hall rocked with the men's laughter. Montsero had achieved instant rapport, Chant thought, and he was suitably impressed.

"So," Montsero continued as the laughter died, "now that the bullshit is out of the way, maybe we can get down to business. It may come as a surprise to you badasses, but a lot of you are in much better shape, physically and mentally, than the good, law-abiding folks out here who've never spent an hour behind any bar that isn't stocked with liquor. It seems that breaking your ass all your life to pay for fancy houses, fast cars, and fast women can be hazardous to your health."

There were loud groans from the men. Montsero stepped down from the platform, paced back and forth for a few moments, then was able to silence the men with a single, curt gesture.

"Some of the reasons for your good health seem self-evident," the psychologist continued as he reached the far end of the hall, turned, and started back. "Assuming you don't get knifed or ass-fucked to death, prison can actually be a fairly easy place to live. You eat, sleep, work, play, and shit on command. If you stay on the right side of the guards, and establish your space with the other prisoners, things tend to go along pretty smoothly. You get plenty of food, sleep, and exercise; you eat three times a day—the food may taste like shit, but it's more of a balanced diet than any of you would eat on your own. You don't do much booze or dope in prison, because most of you can't come up with the necessary cash. Most important, there just aren't a whole hell of a lot of things for you to worry about—until you get outside, where there are too many things to do and you can't, or aren't permitted to, do most of them. The bottom line is that there are more healthy old men in prison than there are outside. Stress kills. Now, we know that there are health differences between long-term convicts and the normal population, and we're trying to find out just how great some of those differences are.

"What we're going to do is measure you, physically and psychologically, and then compare your health profiles with those of straights in your age groups. We're underwritten by a group of insurance companies, which means they're providing the bread that goes into your pockets and mine. They've got plenty of money already, but they want to see if they can't find ways to help everyone live longer so that they can make even more. That's what this little gathering is really all about—long-term ex-convicts laboring to insure larger long-term profits for insurance companies. Now, doesn't that gladden your hearts?"

There was another outburst of laughter, which Montsero allowed to continue for some time. He returned to the lectern, adjusted his aviator glasses. Finally he gestured toward the two student assistants, who still looked decidedly uncomfortable.

"Jane and Paul will pass out questionnaires and a pencil for each of you. These are just some simple questions that give us some idea of your general interests and hobbies. All you have to do is read each question and check the box with the sentence that best tells how you feel about the question. If you don't read too well, move around and try to find someone to help you. The only thing I ask is that you don't copy anyone else's answers. That's important; what we want is a picture of *you*. There are no right or wrong answers, so you don't have to worry about 'passing' the test. You get your hundred bucks just for being here and filling out the questionnaires."

"You read?" the man called Tank whispered.

Chant nodded, and the scar-faced man settled back in his desk as a few of the other men cluttered around the better readers.

Montsero tapped on the lectern for attention, got it. "I have one more thing to say, and I want to get it out of the way up front. Each of you will get your hundred bucks this afternoon. Some—but not all—of you will be invited back for other sessions. If you're not invited back, don't worry about it. And don't think we overlooked you, because we didn't; don't call us, we'll call you. It has nothing to do with passing or failing these tests, and it has nothing to do with you as a man; it just means you're not quite what we're looking for. Also, some of you may not *want* to participate in the tests that come after this one. If any of you feel that you can't take some *real* physical testing, you'll be free to take a walk any time you like, with no hassles. That's the story, and I don't expect to have to repeat it. Any questions?"

There weren't any. Montsero nodded to the student assistants, who proceeded to pass out questionnaires and a pencil to each man.

"Neil, what's this?"

"What's your last name?"

"Olsen."

"Write it down."

Chant put his pencil aside and leafed through the first questionnaire, trying to get an overall feel for the questions. It took him less than a minute to determine that Montsero was a liar, which meant that the research project, which seemed to have gained a great deal of respectability over the years, was probably a lie.

The test had nothing to do with general interests, Chant thought, but was a narrow-band personality-screening instrument which seemed specifically designed to probe for paranoia and sociopathology. Every sixth question appeared to be nothing more than a control query designed to disguise the questionnaire's true intent, and the fourth answers to the sixth questions were meaningless. All of the other questions were tightly focused on antisocial and violent traits.

It also meant that Insolers had lied to him, Chant thought. The way the test was designed, it would be transparent to anyone who knew anything about psychological screening instruments that it was the answer to every question *but* the sixth that mattered.

"Neil, what the hell do they mean by this?"

Chant glanced over to see where Tank's thick, gnarled finger was pointing. "They want to know if you're afraid of ghosts, Tank. Not at all, some of the time, most of the time, or all of the time."

Olsen thought about it, tapping the pencil's eraser against his stained, chipped teeth. "Sometimes," he said at last, and checked the appropriate box.

Chant quickly went through the test, marking the fourth answer to ever sixth question as Duane Insolers had suggested he do.

"What about this one, Neil?"

Chant looked at the question. "They want to know if you've ever thought about fucking a corpse."

"Shit, man! They really get down to it, don't they?!"

"Not at all, some of the—"

"Yeah, I got it. Thanks, Neil."

Chant watched Tank Olsen check off the "some of the time" box, then closed his own booklet and tried to think. If every sixth question was meaningless, it meant that his answers to the other questions would determine whether or not he was invited back to the next session. The real question was whether Montsero was looking for the best or worst of them, and Chant decided that the answer was obvious; bringing the two attractive, young student assistants with him had been a purposeful act on the part of the psychologist, designed to excite the men's sexual fantasies.

Chant went through the questionnaire again. On each of the remaining questions he checked off the box next to the most extreme answer. Then he closed his booklet and turned his attention to helping Tank Olsen and a few of the others.

Insolers contacted him on the morning of the fourth day, and arrangements were made to meet in the afternoon.

"So? How'd it go?"

Chant shrugged. "It was the easiest hundred bucks I've ever made in my life. Montsero talked for a few minutes, had us answer some dumb questions, then paid us off and sent us home. The whole thing didn't take more than an hour and a half."

Insolers, who still exuded a strong medicinal smell, lit one of the Benson & Hedges and dropped the match into the heavy glass ashtray between them. He exhaled, then glanced furtively around the small Greenwich Village restaurant. It was early, not yet five o'clock, and there were only six other people in the dining room. Happy Hour was just getting underway in the bar.

"Do you want something else to eat, Alter? How about some pie?"

Chant shook his head.

"You didn't eat much."

"I ate what I wanted."

"You want a drink?"

"No."

Insolers took two quick drags on his cigarette, stubbed it out. "Did you check the boxes I told you to?"

"Yes."

"What did you think of the tests?"

"What was to think? You told me which answers to check off, so I didn't pay much attention to the other questions."

"But you answered the other questions?"

"Sure. But I just put down whatever came to mind. You must have been right about checking the fourth answer to every sixth question, though, because I've been invited back to the next session. The letter came yesterday."

Insolers nodded slowly as he studied Chant. "Good," he said in a low voice. "What did you think of Dr. Montsero?"

"Comes off like a fag, but I think he's a tough son-of-a-bitch."

"Did you notice anything unusual?"

"In an hour and a half? Maybe if you'd tell me what I'm supposed to be looking for, I could give you an answer."

Insolers shook his head. "Not yet. The important thing is that you made the first cut, so to speak. We'll see what happens from here on out. And you'll keep me posted."

"I don't like being taken for granted, Insolers."

"I don't take you for granted, Neil. I've told you that you're very valuable to us. Do you mind if I call you Neil?"

Chant offered an indifferent shrug.

"Okay, Neil, you can call me Duane. I'd like to ask you a question, and I'd appreciate a straight answer; it's important. Four days ago you told me you weren't angry about what had happened to you. Was that the truth?"

"Are you calling me a liar, Duane?"

"Take it easy, Neil. I think you were lying in that particular case. In fact, I think you're a very, very angry man."

"Wouldn't you be if you'd spent twenty years in prison for a crime you didn't commit? The state is thinking about giving me some money, but there's no way they can pay for those twenty years. Goddam right, I'm angry."

"Sure. And you're just waiting for a chance to get even, right? You've got some debts to pay."

"Maybe."

"If you're so angry at the authorities, why did you agree to meet with me? You know I work for the CIA, which means you're now working for the CIA."

Chant wasn't at all certain what answer Insolers would buy, or what he might be looking for, and so he remained silent.

"Neil, you can trust me. I need an answer. Does it make you feel good to spy on other people? Does it give you a feeling of power?"

"Maybe," Chant said carefully.

"God knows you've had enough people spying on you most of your life, right? This gives you a chance to spy on somebody else for a change. You'll know their secrets, but they won't know yours. Right?"

"My reasons are my own, Duane. You're not paying me to answer personal questions."

"Fair enough," Insolers said evenly as he took some bills from his pocket and laid them on the table. Then he rose and put on his overcoat.

"Any tips for the next session, Duane?"

"Nope. You're on your own now. To tell you the truth, I don't know what Montsero will have you doing next. I'll be anxious to hear your report. I'll be talking to you."

Insolers walked away, and Chant signaled the waitress for another cup of coffee. When it arrived he stirred sugar into the strong brew, started to raise the cup to his lips, then set the cup down when he became aware once more of a strong medicinal odor. He slowly turned in his seat and found himself looking up into the cold brown eyes of Duane Insolers. An unlit cigarette dangled from the man's thin lips.

"I thought you'd left," Chant said casually.

"You know, Neil, something about you bothers me."

"What's that?"

"For one thing, you seem just a bit different from when I talked to you in your room four days ago."

"How so?"

"It's something I can't quite put my finger on. I'm thinking about it. You wouldn't be a ringer, would you?"

"A ringer? What the fuck are you talking about, Insolers? You came to me, remember?"

"I've done a little checking on you. San Quentin?"

"You said you read all the applications. If you read mine, you know I was in Q."

"Funny thing about that. There is a Neil Alter who was recently released from San Quentin, and you pretty much fit his description."

"No shit!" Chant said, and laughed.

"He supposedly went to Florida."

"I changed my mind, decided I'd see what I could make go for myself in New York. What the hell are you getting at, Insolers? You know, I'm already sorry I agreed to meet with you. I don't think I'm going to do it again."

The other man was silent for some time as he studied Chant; if he was disturbed by the threat to cut off communication, he didn't show it. "I just hope you're not trying to bullshit me," he said at last in a low voice. "I've got a good nose for bullshit, a really good nose, and today it's been twitching the whole time I've been talking to you."

Chant sighed heavily with affected exasperation. "Why the hell should I try to bullshit you? For that matter, what would I have to bullshit about?"

"Those are two very good questions, Alter," Insolers replied in the same soft, slightly threatening, tone. "I'll be giving them a lot of thought."

This time Chant tracked the other man with his eyes until Insolers had walked out of the restaurant. Duane Insolers, Chant thought, was not a man he would underestimate.

CHAPTER SEVEN _____

TANK OLSEN WAS also among the eighteen men who had been invited back to the second session. The huge, musclebound man seemed to Chant much more subdued and sullen than when they had first met. Chant made a few attempts to start a conversation, but gave up when it became evident that Olsen did not want to talk to him.

This session had begun at one o'clock in the afternoon, and was still going on at seven-thirty. Except for a half-hour break to eat a dinner prepared by a caterer, the men had been kept busy all day answering several detailed questionnaires on their health and family histories, and undergoing complete physical examinations conducted by two internists and an ophthalmic technician who had been brought in for the occasion. Electrocardiograms and electroencephalograms were given; blood, urine, and stool specimens were taken; each man's chest and stomach were X-rayed; their throats were swabbed; rectums probed; reflexes tested with rubber mallet and machine.

Three men had been told to go home when it was discov-

ered that they had severe health problems—one a blood dis-
order, and the other two diabetes. Throughout the day
Montsero, who was not involved in administering any of the
tests, had wandered through the various rooms, sucking on an
unlit pipe and watching through his reflecting aviator glasses.
The man was constantly humming Christmas carols, although
they were now well into the new year. When there was grum-
bling, he patiently reminded the group that each man was
being paid two hundred and fifty dollars for participating in
the day's battery of testing.

There had been hearing tests, and now they were lined up
in a darkened room waiting for a turn on a machine that tested
for color blindness and visual acuity.

"Get your hands off my fucking balls, you goddam fag."

Chant tensed slightly when he recognized Tank Olsen's
voice; the man was very close behind him.

"I told you to get your hand off my balls!"

Chant's *ninja*-trained senses gave him ample warning time
to escape the blow he knew was coming, but he purposely
waited; to evade too quickly could give Montsero some indication of his true capabilities, and this Chant did not wish to
do. Slowing time in his mind, he continued to wait as the
other man's fist shot through the air toward the back of his
skull, then ducked away at the last instant, absorbing the force
of the blow into the sinewy, powerful muscles in his neck and
shoulders.

Feigning pain and injury, Chant stumbled forward, caromed off the man in front of him, and fell to the floor. He
immediately rolled to his left, feigning clumsiness as he
cringed and protected his head and the back of his neck with
his hands. A booted foot bounced off his right hip, and Chant
kept rolling. He came up against a chair, made a show of
struggling to his feet. Tank Olsen rushed at him, and Chant
dropped to his knees. Olsen tripped over him and fell hard on
the chair, smashing it. Chant got up and backed away until he
came up against a wall, then assumed a defensive stance with
his forearms crossed over his throat and stomach.

Someone had turned up the lights. Chant watched as the heavy-breathing Olsen slowly rose from the floor, kicked aside the debris from the shattered chair, swayed, and rubbed his right shoulder. The other ex-convicts had lined up around the room, and their eyes glittered with excitement. The technician who had been operating the eye-testing equipment had backed into a corner; his face was ashen, and he had bunched his baggy lab coat tightly around him as if it were a suit of armor. Montsero, his eyes as always hidden behind his tinted glasses, stood watching with the other men, his hands thrust casually into his pockets.

Olsen sucked in a deep breath and rushed again. Chant stepped aside at the last moment and drove a straight, hard right into the man's bullet-damaged right shoulder. Olsen grunted with pain, clutched at his shoulder, and slowly sank to his knees, his forehead cracking loudly against the wall where Chant had been standing. Still pretending to be unsteady on his feet, Chant moved a few steps along the wall to his right and waited.

Olsen rose to his feet and proceeded to do exactly what Chant expected, which was to repeat what he had done moments before. Head down and arms spread like elephantine wings, the man came lumbering across the short space between them.

Chant stepped forward in order to shorten the distance between them even more and thus reduce the other man's momentum. He angled his body slightly so as to avoid being butted, then centered his weight and lunged forward to absorb the force of the other man's body, deliberately allowing himself to fall into Olsen's grasp.

Olsen grunted with surprise at what he considered his good fortune. Ignoring the fact that Chant had raised his arms over his head at the last moment, the scar-faced man wrapped his arms around Chant's waist, then lifted Chant off the floor and began to squeeze.

With his arms free, Chant could easily kill or permanently cripple the other man in a fraction of a second. Instead, he

cupped his hands around Olsen's eyes, raised the startled
man's eyelids with his middle fingers and dragged the balls of
his thumbs across the naked surface of the eyeballs. Olsen
howled, as much in terror at the sudden realization of how
easily he could have been blinded, as with pain, and immediately released his grip. Chant landed lightly on the balls of his
feet and stepped back as Olsen, hands over his burning eyes,
staggered around in a circle before finally dropping to his
knees.

It would be a simple matter to finish off the man with a fist
or knee, but Chant decided that Neil Alter might well want
someone besides Tank Olsen to pay dearly for this particular
test, which had apparently been designed expressly for him—
even if it were only an insurance company. He walked quickly
across the room and picked up the piece of ophthalmic testing
equipment, walked back, and dropped the heavy device on
Olsen's back, between the shoulder blades. Man and machine
collapsed to the floor, the man unconscious and the complex
but fragile piece of equipment splintering into a thousand
shards of expensive ground lenses, plastic, and metal.

Chant slowly turned to face the others in the room. Brute
force was one thing these men understood; believing that this
was what they had witnessed, there were quiet grunts of surprise, approval, and respect from the circle of ex-convicts.
Montsero had not moved, and his face revealed nothing. His
hands were still in his pockets, and the unlit pipe still jutted
from his mouth.

"You can take that out of my pay," Chant said to Montsero
as he pointed to the shattered machine.

Two men quickly stepped aside as Chant walked between
them and out the door.

Chant walked across the street from the Blake College campus
and waited in the darkness. Twenty minutes later all of the
men in the group except Tank Olsen emerged from the main
building; they were laughing and joking, and in the light cast
by the mercury-vapor lamps ringing the campus Chant could

see that they were taking turns mimicking the way he had dropped the testing machine on Olsen's back.

Olsen came out fifteen minutes later. He was limping badly, and he paused just outside the exit to rub his eyes. He put both hands in the small of his back, stretched and groaned loudly, then continued limping down the sidewalk to the street. He turned right and headed toward the subway station four blocks away. Chant followed, walking on the narrow strip of grass between the sidewalk and street in order to muffle his footsteps.

Next to the campus was a vest-pocket park in which all of the lights had been broken by rocks or BB pellets. Now Chant quickly closed the distance between himself and the other man. Suddenly sensing Chant's presence, Olsen started to turn; but by then Chant had already crashed into Olsen's side, bumping the other man into the darkness of the park. Olsen staggered, finally regained his balance, and swung a wild roundhouse right at the shadowy figure in front of him. Chant leaned back just far enough to allow the gnarled fist to pass in front of his face, then lashed out with a precisely aimed front kick that caught Olsen squarely in the solar plexus. The air exploded from the ex-convict's lungs; his eyes bulged from his head as he grasped his belly, bent over double, then sat down hard on the cold, cracked concrete. His face immediately began to turn blue.

Chant squatted down next to the big man. "Lie back, Tank," he said quietly, gently pressing with his left palm against Olsen's chest while with the other hand he reached down and gripped the man's belt. "Try to relax. I'll help you breathe."

Still wide-eyed, Olsen allowed himself to be pushed on his back while he stared up into Chant's face. With recognition came fear, but he did not move as Chant lifted his midsection by the belt and gently massaged an area just below his rib cage.

"I'm sorry I had to hurt you again, Tank," Chant continued in the same soft, even tone, "but I had to get your attention.

What was that all about in there? Who told you to unload on me?"

Olsen shook his head. He was beginning to breathe regularly. Suddenly his right hand bunched into a fist that shot toward Chant's head. Chant casually blocked the blow, then jabbed the stiffened three middle fingers of his right hand into Olsen's midsection. The man's eyes rolled back into his head as his chest heaved and he again began to gasp for air. Chant steadied him, massaged his diaphragm.

"We can do this all night, my friend," Chant said, "but I don't see the point in your having to suffer. Answer my questions, and I won't do that again. Did Montsero sic you on me?"

Olsen, shuddering with the effort to breathe, looked down at the fingers poised over his stomach. He grimaced as if in anticipation of the next blow, shook his head.

"Who, then?"

"Can't . . . tell."

Chant tapped Olsen's stomach softly with the tips of his fingers. The man yelped, drew his knees up to his stomach and stuttered something that might have been a name.

"Who?"

"Ah, ah, ah . . . In . . . Insolers. Man named Insolers."

Chant quickly looked away to hide any reaction that might show on his face. When he turned back, he found that Olsen had rolled away from him and was huddled on the icy concrete, his knees clutched to his chest. Chant reached out and gently gripped the man's shoulders.

"Who's this Insolers, Tank?"

Tank shook his head again.

"Come on, my friend," Chant said as he moved the fingers of his right hand from Olsen's shoulder to his windpipe. "Don't you like breathing?"

"You're fast, man," Olsen whispered in a curiously childlike voice. "And you hurt."

"Answer the question. Who's this Insolers?"

"CIA agent," Tank Olsen mumbled.

Chant straightened up and stood over the other man. "What would a CIA agent want with you?"

"He came to me, asked me to help him; said something funny was going on with Montsero and the group. He wanted me to keep an eye on things and report back to him."

Chant wondered if Insolers, or someone like him, had contacted every man in the group; he strongly suspected that was the case. "Why did he choose you?"

"He said the CIA had investigated me, and they thought I was the best man for the job."

"What were you supposed to look for?"

"He never said. I was just supposed to watch what went on."

"Why were you told to attack me?"

"I don't know why; I was just told to do it." Now the big man sat up and lifted his face toward Chant. In the moonlight, Chant could see tears glistening in Olsen's scar-framed eyes. "I didn't want to, Neil. I liked you. But I had to follow orders."

"It's all right. I understand."

"You a Russian spy?"

"No."

"It don't make no difference; I still blew it. Shit. I liked working for the CIA."

"Don't worry about it, Tank. You're still working for us."

"When Duane finds out I . . . Huh?"

"I'm not a Russian agent, Tank; I'm CIA. Duane Insolers works for me."

"You? But why—?"

"You can't become a CIA agent just like that, Tank. I had to test you; I had to see how loyal you were, and if you'd follow orders. Duane was acting on my instructions when he ordered you to attack me."

"Holy shit," Olsen murmured as he scratched his head.

"You followed orders well enough, but you failed the most important test. You should never have told me the truth just now. You know that, don't you?"

"What was I supposed to do, let you kill me?"

"I wasn't going to kill you," Chant replied evenly. "I didn't even come close. All I did was knock the wind out of you a couple of times."

"Yeah, well, that doesn't feel too good, you know," Olsen mumbled.

"You think just anybody can become a CIA agent? You should have been able to take a lot more punishment than I gave you before telling me about Duane. I must admit that I'm a little surprised at how easy it was for me to force you to talk. Maybe we were wrong about you."

"Shit," Olsen said quietly, dropping his gaze. "Sorry, Neil. I'm really ashamed of myself."

"Look at me, Tank," Chant said. He waited until Olsen glanced up at him, then reached down and gripped the man's good shoulder. "I'm going to give you another chance."

The big man smiled tentatively. "You are?"

"Yes. It was probably unfair of us to expect you to hold out under torture without more training. I still think you're the right man; I think you're going to make a good agent as soon as you get a little more experience."

"Damn, I *know* I will! Thanks, Neil. This is the first decent job I've ever had. I just wish my parents were alive and could know; they'd be proud of me."

"But another chance means another test."

Olsen winced and quickly put his hands over his stomach. "What kind of test?"

"All you have to do is keep your mouth shut, Tank—like you should have done this time."

Olsen took his hands away from his stomach and breathed a small sigh of relief. "I will, Neil. You can count on me."

"What happened just now stays between us; the fact that you told me about you and Duane working for the CIA is our secret. You don't even tell Duane; that's very important. Don't mention anything to *anyone* about this little chat we're having."

Tank Olsen's battered face wrinkled into a puzzled frown. "How come?"

"First, Duane might not agree with my decision to give you another chance; he might go over my head to try to get you taken off this operation. Second, we think there's a good possibility that *Duane* is working for the Russians."

"Jesus Christ," Olsen said, his eyes going wide.

"Spying is a complicated business, my friend. You'll understand that when you've been at it as long as I have. Just follow my orders, and you'll stay a CIA agent. Report to Duane like you're supposed to; tell him about the fight at the college, but not about this talk. On the other hand, you'll report to *me* everything Duane says to *you*. Have you got it?"

Olsen nodded eagerly. "I got it."

"You think you can pull it off, keep the fact that you and I are working together a secret?"

"I can do it."

"Insolers isn't stupid, you know. I don't want him reading things in your face or voice. I don't want to see you kicked out of the CIA, and I don't want Insolers to know that we're on to the fact that he may be working for the Russians."

"I can do it, Neil."

"I know you can. Now, Montsero may not invite either of us back after what happened—but I have a strong hunch he will. If he does, you have to remember that you're supposed to be mad at me. Stay away from me. I'll signal you if I want to meet and talk; you signal me—*subtly*—if you've spoken with Duane."

"I can handle it, Neil. Thanks for giving me a second chance."

Chant extended his hand to Olsen, helped the man to his feet. "You all right?"

Olsen rubbed his stomach. He tentatively sucked in a deep breath, then nodded his head.

"Remember, Tank, not a word to anyone," Chant continued. "You're my man now; you report only to me."

"Thanks, Neil!" Olsen called as Chant turned and walked out of the small park. "Thanks a lot!"

Insolers contacted him a week later.

"So? How'd it go this time?"

Chant slowly glanced around the Village restaurant, the same one where they had met the first time, then leaned across the table. "I'm a little concerned, Duane," he said in a low voice.

Insolers, uncharacteristically dressed casually in jeans and a hooded gray sweatshirt, narrowed his eyes and leaned back, as if Chant's closeness were offensive to him. The medicinal smell that seemed to perpetually hover about the man was even stronger this evening. "Why is that, Neil?"

"I think the people we're after may be on to me."

"Why do you say that?"

"This big guy jumped me at the last session. He said I'd put my hand on his balls."

"So? Did you put your hand on his balls?"

Chant affected a pained expression. *"No,* Duane. That's what I 'm trying to tell you; the guy had no reason to come after me. Do you think maybe he's one of them?"

"One of whom?"

"One of the Russian agents."

"I never said anything about Russian agents."

"No, but I can read between the lines. You just said to keep my eyes and ears open, but why would the CIA want me in there if not to look for enemy agents?"

Insolers, his eyes searching Chant's face, grunted noncommittally, said nothing.

"You think this guy was ordered to kill me, Duane?"

"If he was ordered to kill you, he certainly fucked up, didn't he? I don't see a scratch on you. What'd you do, beat the shit out of him?"

Chant shrugged. "He was a big son-of-a-bitch, but pretty slow; too much muscle in too many of the wrong places."

"Still, it occurs to me that you must be one hell of a street fighter—or maybe just one hell of a fighter, period."

"I guess I can hold my own; to survive twenty years in prison, you have to learn to hold your own. I'm just glad I didn't fuck up our deal—my parents would be proud of the fact that I'm working for the CIA. I was afraid Montsero wouldn't invite me back after the fight, but he did. I got my letter two days ago."

Insolers's eyes kept searching Chant's face. "I'm glad to hear that, Neil," he said quietly.

"I'll tell you this, though: I'm going to get even with that big, ambushing son-of-a-bitch when this is over. I'm going to set up a little ambush of my own—one he won't walk away from so easily."

"When this is over, you can do anything you like."

"You still haven't answered my question, Duane. Do you think somebody wants to kill me because they're on to the fact that I'm working for you?"

Insolers shook his head. "I think this guy who jumped you just had his balls squeezed and thought you did it. If an enemy power wanted to take you out, don't you think they'd have found someone who'd do the job right?"

Chant pretended to think about it, finally nodded. "I guess you're right. I didn't think of that."

"You're new in the business. Don't be too hard on yourself."

"Well, I want to learn." Chant placed his hands flat on the table, shook his head. "You know, Duane, one thing really puzzles me."

"What puzzles you?"

"What would the Russians—or any enemy government for that matter—want with a bunch of long-term ex-convicts?" Chant waited, but the question was greeted by silence. Finally he looked up from the backs of his hands into the cold, brown eyes of the man sitting across from him. "Do you know, Duane?"

Insolers, his gaze locked with Chant's, still said nothing.

"I mean, think about it," Chant continued. "I'm the only

guy in that group who isn't totally fucked up. At the first session, at least, there were what seemed like some regular guys, but they're gone. Shit, Duane; except for me, the only guys left are really fucking crazy."

"No offense, Neil," Insolers said carefully, "but Montsero obviously thinks you have something in common with the others, or he wouldn't have invited you back. Maybe you managed to convince him that you're as crazy as the rest of them."

"Well, I'm not," Chant said, very much aware of the fact that as the group became increasingly more selective, he had increasingly less room to maneuver in his role as Neil Alter. "Most of those other guys will either be dead or back in prison inside a year. They're garbage; any one of them would knife you for the change in your pocket. Nobody can predict what they're going to do. What possible use could they be to anybody?"

Insolers lit a cigarette. His movements were very slow and deliberate—a mask, Chant was certain, for the furious racing of his mind.

"There are still some things I can't tell you," Insolers replied at last, a low hum of tension in his voice. "Like I said, you're new to this business; you'll need a lot more experience before you can be fully briefed on any mission. You wouldn't want to tip our hand to anyone, would you?"

"I'd never do that, Duane."

"Not intentionally. But you wouldn't want to risk doing it unintentionally, either. Right?"

"No. I wouldn't want to do that."

"I'm glad to hear it," Insolers said, rising and putting on his coat.

"Hey, I told you about the fight, but you haven't even asked me what else went on at the second session. Don't you want to know?"

"Sure," Insolers said as he dropped a twenty-dollar bill on the table to pay for their food. His voice was distant, as if he was distracted by other things on his mind. "What else went on?"

"Except for the fight, nothing unusual—at least nothing that seemed unusual to me. There were a couple more questionnaires, but they were short. Then we spent a lot of time getting checked out by doctors. I'll tell you, my ass is still sore from—"

"Keep up the good work, Neil," Insolers said curtly, then turned and walked out of the restaurant.

CHAPTER EIGHT _____

THE ELEVEN MEN left in the group were taken to an abandoned Army base in upstate New York for a series of arduous physical trials. To himself, Chant called them names such as *the run, field of fire and fangs,* and *the pit;* and they were the ultimate physical tests that Montsero could devise—competitions made even more grueling by the grimness and ferocity of the men who took part in them. After the field trials, seven men had been brought back to Blake College, to a different, smaller room.

To pain.

The electricity coursed through Chant's body like some huge, acid-skinned snake burrowing in his veins and between his muscles, locking his joints and arching his spine. The pain writhed for a few seconds in the pit of his stomach, then stopped.

Montsero sat twenty feet away in a straight-backed wooden chair. On a table next to him was the apparatus that generated and delivered the electricity in random bursts of steadily increasing voltage. Although they were facing each other, Montsero never looked up at Chant; the psychologist intently studied the dials on the machine, then quickly made notes on a long, yellow legal pad when a meter indicated that a charge had been delivered. Flashing lights from the various dials, meters, and other monitoring devices were eerily reflected across the dark surface of the man's aviator glasses.

Cut into the wall behind and above the psychologist's head was a large, square mirror; there was no doubt in Chant's mind that the mirror was two-way, and that behind the glass sat the individual whose hidden presence he had first sensed during the field trials, the individual Chant had come to think of as the Watcher.

Chant assumed it was Insolers, who had not contacted him since their second meeting.

Another shock came, knifing through his bowels and genitals, flashing up through his stomach and into his chest. Chant suppressed the urge to vomit, then forced himself to turn his thoughts elsewhere so as not to waste energy in trying to anticipate when the next shock would come.

Another jolt flashed through him, and he bucked in the chair. He knew that he had already surpassed the pain levels endured by the other men, but wanted to score as high as he possibly could. He assumed that Montsero would stop the test before the machine generated a shock powerful enough to do physical damage; however, he could not be certain of this, and after another shock that clenched his jaws shut and made his eyeballs roll back in his head he abruptly stood up, breaking contact with the electrodes planted in the arms, legs, seat, and back of the sweat- and urine-stained leather chair in which the subjects sat.

"That's it," Chant said evenly.

"First of all," Montsero said tightly, "I'd like to congratulate you seven men on completing the entire battery of tests in the experimental project. It takes some big balls to stay in this group until the end, and I think it's only proper that you should be suitably rewarded."

The psychologist seemed uncharacteristically nervous and unsure of himself, Chant thought, and he wondered why. Despite their much smaller number, they were assembled in the large lecture hall where the group had first met, with Chant and the others dressed in the navy blue jumpsuits they had been issued at the beginning of the field trials. Montsero, dressed in a charcoal-gray suit, stood at the lectern at the front of the hall, leafing through a stack of papers with quick, bird-like motions.

"The testing is finished, gentlemen," Montsero continued. "However, we're not finished with you; I'm about to make a proposal which I think all of you will find most attractive." The psychologist paused and, for the first time since he had been with the group, removed his glasses to clean them, revealing large, protruding eyeballs. He put the glasses back on, then nervously licked his lips before going on. "First, though, there's another matter to be dealt with. Mr. Alter, will you please step into the room behind me? There's someone who'd like to speak with you."

Chant experienced a sudden premonition of danger. However, he rose without hesitation from his seat and walked past the lectern to the door directly behind Montsero. He turned the knob and stepped into what turned out to be a small, windowless office. Then he grunted softly, and slowly closed the door behind him. Unfortunately, Chant thought, his charade was over.

It was certain that Neil Alter was about to be summarily expelled from the group, and possible that he would be summarily executed.

Although two decades had passed since Chant had last seen him, the man sitting behind the desk in the office was instantly recognizable. He had a heavily scarred, triangular-shaped face with a fleshy lump for a nose, which had been broken far too many times to ever be reset properly. There

were scars on his patchy scalp where hair had been torn out by
dying men locked in a deadly embrace, and the graying tufts
that were left were worn long and combed back over his head.
His green eyes were unnaturally bright—intelligent, reptile-
cruel, and quite insane.

Standing, the other man would be just under six feet, with
a barrel chest and thick legs evident even under his finely
tailored suit. However, despite his brawn and manifest ugli-
ness, the man's most striking physical feature would be his
arms—powerful, like the rest of his body, but grotesquely
extended, almost simianlike in their length, to a point only a
few inches above his knees.

According to Army legend, Tommy Wing had acquired his
nickname as a fifteen-year-old juvenile offender in Otisville,
New York State's maximum-security facility for minors;
clubbed into semiconsciousness by two guards intent on rape,
and forced to perform fellatio on one, Wing had proceeded to
bite off the man's penis. Unlike Tank Olsen, Chant thought,
whose mutilated face was the result of poor fighting technique, Tommy Wing's ruined features were a matter of choice,
the price he casually paid for a particular style of combat that
was devastatingly effective on both the bodies and minds of
his hapless opponents: Wing was a biter. His octopus arms
and powerful buck teeth were the only weapons he cared to
use. Like some mindless fighting machine that did not feel
pain, Wing would absorb any degree of punishment necessary
to get him inside the circle of an opponent's flailing fists; once
there, Tommy Wing would use his long arms to grasp the
opponent to him. And then he would begin to chew.

Even after twenty years, Chant well remembered the sensation of Wing's teeth grinding in his flesh during their terrible
battle; among the many scars Hammerhead had left on his
body, there was a huge, ragged one on his right calf where the
man's teeth had come within millimeters of severing his
Achilles tendon and permanently crippling him.

"Well, well, well," Tommy Wing said, his lips drawing

back from his teeth in a hideous grimace. "John Sinclair, of all people."

There was no other chair in the room, so Chant eased himself down on a corner of the large desk, noting with satisfaction that the other man—despite the .45 automatic he held in his hand—moved back slightly. "The name's Alter, pal. Who the hell are you?"

"I ain't your fairy godmother, Sinclair, and that's for sure. Don't try to bullshit me. I've been watching you for better than a month. You disguise your moves pretty well, but they're still your moves. Also, I've seen you stripped. Don't you think I'd remember the marks I put on you? How the hell did you get wind of this?"

"Get wind of what, Tommy?" Chant asked casually, gauging the distance between himself and the gun, deciding that the desk between them—combined with Hammerhead's insensitivity to pain and uncanny capacity to absorb a blow—weighted the odds too heavily in the other man's favor. In the present situation, he would make a move only if he was certain Wing was about to pull the trigger.

"What the hell are you doing here? How did you get wind of this setup?"

"I don't know what you're talking about, Tommy," Chant replied, casually removing his wig and contact lenses, setting the items down next to him on the desk. "I got here the same way as everybody else. I've spent the last twenty years in prison. I changed my name, decided to change my appearance to go along with it."

"What bullshit," Hammerhead said, and laughed. "You've spent the last twenty years making life miserable for some very powerful and wealthy men—and becoming very wealthy yourself, in the process."

"You seem to know a lot about me, Tommy."

"Damn straight, Sinclair. And with all the people around the fucking world after your ass, look who's got you. I like that."

"I heard you were in a mental hospital, Tommy. How in hell did you get out of there? Did you do a good job brushing your teeth three times a day?"

Hammerhead's bright green eyes glinted, and his free hand bunched into a fist. "You're the only man who's ever beaten me, Sinclair—you and those goddam funny moves of yours. I was in the infirmary a month longer than you; they had to remove a kidney and four feet of intestine to stop the internal bleeding, and cut off my left nut to boot."

"Look on the bright side of things, Tommy," Chant said in a flat voice. "You got a free lunch; you must have chewed off at least a pound of flesh. That's not bad pickings for an amateur cannibal."

Color rose in the other man's pronounced cheekbones. "You've got a bad mouth, Sinclair; always did."

"And you were always a terrific straight man. But I'm not going to touch that line; it's too easy."

"You should have killed me when you had the chance."

"Hell, Tommy, I thought I had."

"I asked you what you're doing here, Sinclair, and I'm still waiting for an answer."

"Maybe I'm after your job. From the looks of that suit you're wearing, it pays well. I assume being locked up in a mental hospital for twenty years qualified you for this project. Did you come up through the ranks?"

"It'll be a cold day in hell when you get my job, Sinclair; nobody's going to hire a corpse. And when Mr. Blake finds out who I've got for him, I suspect I'll be in for a pretty good raise."

Chant felt his stomach muscles tighten slightly, and suddenly he understood how Tommy Wing had come to know so much about him. "So Blake College is named after *that* Blake," he said, raising his eyebrows slightly. "How interesting."

Hammerhead frowned. "You didn't know that?"

"Tommy, there must be a hundred Blakes in the Manhattan directory alone. How is R. Edgar these days?"

"Still thoroughly pissed about that two million you stole
from him. If you didn't know about Blake's connection to this
college, what are you doing here? I think you're full of shit."

"How did you get hooked up with R. Edgar Blake,
Tommy? Blake has dozens of top-flight professional killers on
his payroll, so what would he want with you? Is he into hiring
the handicapped these days?"

The blood drained from Tommy Wing's face, and he swallowed hard. "Figuring out how I want to kill you, and then
doing it, is going to give me real pleasure, Sinclair."

"Oh, hell, Tommy, we both know *you'd* love to nibble me
to death. But if I were you, I'd check with R. Edgar first to
see what *he* wants to do with me."

"How'd you find out about this project?!"

"Have R. Edgar give me a call, Tommy. I'll tell him."

"Somebody had to help you get in here, Sinclair. Who was
it? Who knows you're doing this thing?"

Chant felt something thick and cold begin to crawl up his
spine: fear. "I've penetrated organizations a lot tighter than
this one without any help, Tommy," he said evenly. "If you
know so much about me, then you know I always work alone.
Now, why don't you tell me what the program is really all
about? What's going on here?"

Hammerhead raised the automatic, pointed it directly at
Chant's forehead. "I think it might be to everyone's advantage
if I killed you right now," he said in a low voice.

"You think R. Edgar will be happy if you do that, Tommy?
I'm not so sure.. I wouldn't want anything bad to happen to
you."

Hammerhead's response was to reach to his left with his
free hand and press a button on an intercom built into the wall.

"Yes?" It was Montsero's voice; the psychologist sounded
even more nervous than before.

"Come get the son-of-a-bitch, you idiot. This way you can
see what he really looks like."

Chant turned his head when he heard the door open behind
him, found himself looking at his own reflection in Mont-

sero's aviator glasses. The psychologist, too, was holding a large automatic.

"Did he tell you anything?" Montsero's voice was high-pitched, and cracked at the end.

Tommy Wing shook his head.

Montsero swallowed hard, licked his lips. "We have to know how he got here, and whom he may have spoken to about us. Can't we do something to make him talk?"

Hammerhead's laugh was loud and ugly. "Like what? You're looking at a man who'll die before he tells you anything he doesn't want you to know."

"Who *is* he, Mr. Wing?"

"None of your goddam business. *What* he is is somebody who has no business being here. That's *your* responsibility, Montsero."

The psychologist, upset and clearly frightened, took off his glasses. His protruding eyeballs seemed even larger. "Mr. Wing, it's not my fault. He was referred here, just like all the others. There was nothing unusual...I had no way of knowing...I checked everything on his application, all of it. It was—"

"Shut up, idiot," Hammerhead said curtly. "The bottom line is that he fooled you. Did you tell the men what I told you to tell them?"

"Yes, sir," Montsero whispered hoarsely.

"Good. What we're going to do is find a place to lock up Mr. Sinclair until I can get a call through to Switzerland. Then I want a look at the application this man filled out, and I especially want a look at the referral sheet."

"That's no problem, sir. No problem at all."

"This isn't your style, Tommy," Chant said softly, easing himself off the desk and looking directly into the emerald green eyes. The fear had crawled all the way up his spine and was now wrapping itself around his neck. "If you want me killed, do it yourself. Let's go one more time, man to man, for old time's sake. I've picked up some new moves you might like to see."

Hammerhead's green eyes suddenly glowed even brighter. "Sinclair, I'd like nothing better than to take you apart—which I just may do in a few minutes." He paused, turned to Montsero and nodded toward the door. "Take him into the other room and wait for me. And watch your ass. If you think he's fooled you so far, you haven't seen anything until he makes a move on you; this is the fastest man with his hands and feet you're ever likely to meet."

"Mr. Wing, are you going to tell Mr. Blake—?"

"Shut up. What I tell Mr. Blake is also none of your business. On second thought, we won't lock him up; with Sinclair, it's better to have him where you can see him. Just take him into the other room and sit him down in a chair. Have the other men stay away from him, and you keep your distance—stay at least ten feet away from him, and keep your gun aimed right on the center of his chest. If he twitches the wrong way, blow his heart out. We can't be faulted for stopping him from escaping, and it's probably what we'll be told to do anyway."

Montsero quickly backed out of the doorway and Chant found himself looking out into the lecture hall. Tank Olsen looked extremely uncomfortable and uncertain, while the faces of the other men—with the exception of Chuck Politan—were cold, hard, and accusing. Chant followed slowly after the man, confident now of escape despite the fact that Montsero had moved a good twenty feet away. Montsero was not Hammerhead, Chant thought; from the way the psychologist held his automatic, it was obvious that the man was not used to firearms. He would freeze for a split second, and that split second was all Chant needed to dive, roll, and come up under the man's aim, It was only a matter of waiting a few moments until Hammerhead had busied himself with his overseas call.

"Get away from those other men, spy," Montsero said from where he was standing near the first tier of seats. "I want you over here, sitting down. Move it."

"I'm coming, Montsero," Chant said, casually stepping down off the raised platform and walking across the well of the lecture hall, angling ever so slightly in the psychologist's direction. "I'll do what you say; just don't get an itchy trigger finger."

Now, he thought.

"I said you could count on me, Neil! I'll get the bastard!"

To Chant's dismay, Tank Olsen suddenly lurched forward and came lumbering down off the platform, head down and arms outstretched, heading straight for Montsero. The psychologist started, then swung the gun slightly to his left in order to fire a bullet into the head of the ex-convict.

By his lies, Chant thought, he had made Tank Olsen's life his responsibility. The man was throwing away his life to save a supposed CIA agent. Although the distraction created by Olsen's sudden and unexpected movement would make it even easier for him to get to Montsero, Chant was not certain he could do it before the psychologist pulled the trigger—and he could not allow the huge child-man to die for him.

As Olsen swept past him, Chant leaped forward and hit him at the knees with his shoulder. Olsen did a complete flip in the air, landed hard on his back. In a single motion, Chant kept rolling, came up and hit Olsen on the chin with his fist, knocking the other man unconscious.

"Big, dumb son-of-a-bitch," Chant said, shaking his head as he slowly got to his feet. He could only hope that the psychologist had not heard Olsen's words. "He must have really taken a dislike to me, Montsero. He was afraid you were going to shoot me before he had a chance to kill me with his bare hands."

Montsero, mouth open and gun shaking in his trembling hand, said nothing. Chant heard a sound behind him, and turned to face Hammerhead, who had rushed out of the office and was now standing in a crouch, his legs braced slightly apart, his automatic raised and aimed with both hands at Chant's head. From the expression on Tommy Wing's face, Chant knew the other man had not been fooled—and now his chance to escape was gone.

"You've got ringers all over the fucking place, stupid," Hammerhead spat at the psychologist. "See if you can get this right: come up and put the gun right at the base of his skull. If he moves his head at all, blow his brains out."

Montsero did as he was told. As he felt the cold metal touch the back of his neck, Chant flexed his knees slightly and watched with the other men as Hammerhead slowly came down into the well, stopped in front of him. There was nothing Chant could do as the hand with the gun suddenly shot out and the barrel slammed into the side of his head, just above the temple. Chant tried to kick at the other man, but the strength in his legs was gone. He put his hands to his head, then sank slowly down into a vast sea of shimmering, orange-streaked pain.

CHAPTER NINE _____

THERE WOULD BE no getting up from the torture chair this
time, Chant thought. Leather straps around his ankles, wrists,
and chest held him securely, with just enough play in the right
wrist strap to allow his hand to reach the red button on the
newly installed console beside him.

"Gentlemen," Montsero said, his voice high-pitched with
excitement, "you will now have the privilege of participating
in an unscheduled but very interesting experiment. We are
going to see how far the bond of loyalty between the two of
you will stretch. You feel the electricity already. We're beginning at a low voltage level, which will steadily increase. In a
very short time both of you will feel considerable discomfort;
soon after that, you will begin to scream. Either one of you
can end the agony simply by pressing the red button next to
you; that will kill the man sitting in the other chair, and then
cut off the electricity. Very simple. Of course, things could be
made even simpler if Mr. Sinclair would just tell us what we
want to know. Then you could both live."

Chant, who had been allowing his mind to float idly in his

wa, his warm sea of good memories, now opened his eyes and looked at Montsero, who was sitting in a chair behind the table with the electrical-discharge apparatus. Hammerhead was standing directly behind the psychologist, feet slightly apart and hands thrust into the pockets of his expensive, Italian-cut slacks. Hammerhead's cold eyes were as vacant as the reflective surface of Montsero's glasses.

"Hey, man! Shit! Whoever the hell you are, tell them what they want to know!"

Chant casually glanced to his right, where Tank Olsen was strapped into an identical chair that had been installed a few feet away. Olsen's face glistened with sweat, and his eyes bulged with terror.

"There isn't anything to tell them, Tank," Chant said quietly. "Try to relax and remember the pleasant things that have happened in your life. Dying isn't anywhere near as important as you think it is."

"Tell them about you and me and the CIA!"

"Haven't you already told them everything there is to tell?"

"They don't believe me!"

"They believe you, Tank. I'm not with the CIA, and they know that. I lied to you. I'm sorry."

"Tell them about Insolers!"

"Insolers is one of them. Insolers contacted every man in the group and told him the same story. He wanted to see how we'd react. It was part of the experiment."

Olsen tilted his head forward, straining against the leather straps until the veins in his neck bulged and his face turned crimson. "What do you *want?!*" he screamed at the two silent, watching men.

"Mostly, they just want to kill me, Tank," Chant said evenly. "They're going to kill you because you tried to help me."

"But you *tricked* me, for Christ's sake! Can't they understand that?!"

"They understand it; it just doesn't make any difference to them. The fact that you transferred your loyalty to someone else in the group makes you useless to them, and you know too much. Also, these guys are sadists; it's how they get their rocks off. I got you into this, Tank. I'm sorry you have to die, but there's absolutely nothing I can do about it. If I could trade my life for yours, I would; but they want you dead for their own reasons. The best you can do is to deny these bastards the satisfaction you're giving them now. Nothing you or I can say is going to make any difference, so you may as well tell them to go fuck themselves." Chant paused, shifted his gaze to Montsero and Hammerhead. "Gentlemen, go fuck yourselves."

The muscles in Montsero's jaws clenched, but Tommy Wing merely flashed his hideous, merciless grin. Chant caught a movement out of the corner of his eye, and he again looked to his right. Olsen, perhaps fully realizing for the first time what the red button was supposed to do, had his hand poised over it.

"I'm not going to press my button, Tank," Chant said easily, speaking to the question in the other man's terrified eyes. "I'm simply going to wait to die, and whether you kill me or they kill me is of monumental indifference to me. You must make your own decision as to what you're going to do in the last moments of your life. I can't advise you, except to say that I don't think pushing that button is going to make a damn bit of difference; we're still both going to die. Montsero and the cannibal are just playing games with your head."

Olsen said something in reply, but Chant was no longer listening. The current running through his body was not yet strong enough to cause real pain, but the muscles in his arms, legs, and stomach were beginning to twitch involuntarily, and he wished only to retreat back into the pleasure of his *wa* and wait there until he ceased to exist. His fate was now irrevocably in the hands of others, and what happened—or when— was no longer of interest to him.

The last thing he glimpsed with his peripheral vision was Tank Olsen's trembling hand descending toward the red button on his console.

CHAPTER TEN _____

CHANT REGAINED CONSCIOUSNESS to the fetid smell of blood, vomit, and viscera. He opened his eyes, immediately understood Hammerhead's parting grin: Tommy Wing clearly had a grisly plan of revenge marked out—a plan far worse for Chant than mere death.

Tank Olsen and Montsero had been butchered by someone very strong, like Hammerhead, wielding something heavy and razor-sharp, perhaps a machete. Bloody chunks of both men were strewn about the room, and their severed heads had been placed alongside each other on top of the electrical discharge apparatus; Montsero's aviator glasses had been neatly set in place on the bridge of his nose.

Chant imagined he could almost hear the echo of Hammerhead's loud, mad laughter ringing in the room.

The straps on the torture chair had been unbuckled, but Chant did not immediately rise. He sat still, scanning the small lecture hall with his eyes as he tried to make sense of what had happened, and why he was still alive. Hammerhead, he thought, had undoubtedly killed Montsero because of what Hammerhead considered the psychologist's lax security measures. In addition, probably without Montsero's knowing it, Hammerhead must have rigged the discharge apparatus so that Olsen would die, but Chant would only be stunned into unconsciousness.

Why? Some kind of macabre joke?

Chant continued to mull it over in his mind, until the answer came to him with a stunning impact that left a burning taste in the back of his mouth that had nothing to do with the electricity that had coursed through his body.

His watch had been taken from him before he'd been strapped into the chair, but a clock on the wall read seven-thirty; he'd been unconscious close to three hours.

He hoped he was not too late.

Chant rose from the chair, walked quickly down into the well of the lecture room, up onto the platform to the door of the office where he had met with Hammerhead. The door was locked, but Chant kicked it open. In three quick strides he was across the office and behind the desk. There was a telephone and a Manhattan directory in one of the drawers, and Chant quickly dialed Martha Greenblatt's number. There was no answer. After fifteen rings Chant hung up, found Jan Rawlings's home number in the Manhattan directory, called that. Again, there was no answer.

Although he was out of disguise and the jumpsuit he was wearing was splattered with blood, Chant knew there was no time to do anything about it. If Martha Greenblatt and Jan Rawlings were still alive, Chant thought, it would only be because Hammerhead had underestimated how long he would be unconscious. Minutes could count.

He hurried from the building and across the campus. He broke into the first car he found, crossed the wires, and within moments was on his way into Manhattan. Traffic was light, and in less than half an hour he had pulled up to the curb in front of Martha Greenblatt's East Side brownstone. Chant leaped out of the car, bounded up the steps to the entrance.

Lights were on inside the brownstone, but there was no answer to his knock. When the knob didn't turn, Chant kicked the door open and stepped into the richly decorated vestibule. His first reaction was relief, for there was no blood; then the smell came to him.

Searching through tears, Chant found the mutilated bodies of Martha and Harry Greenblatt in the blood-drenched master bedroom. Martha's severed head had been placed on top of her typewriter, which in turn was set in the middle of a small writing desk placed in a corner of the bedroom. Her silver hair was stained crimson, and her pale eyes stared unseeing through the lenses of her reading glasses.

"I'm so sorry, Martha," Chant said aloud, wiping away tears. He found two silk scarves in the dresser drawer, covered the heads, sighed deeply. "You turned out to be too good a lawyer for both of us; I never should have listened to you. But you won't be forgotten, and the men who did this won't be forgiven. I promise you they'll pay."

With that, Chant took the grief in his heart and gently pushed it aside to where it could be treated another day, but would not now dull his senses or interfere with what he had to do.

There was a blood-stained piece of paper lying on the floor near the writing stand, and Chant picked it up. It was a carbon copy of a letter, apparently left on the floor as "evidence."

Dear Sirs,
 It has recently come to my attention that a man taking part in experiments at Blake College under the name of Neil Alter is actually the criminal, John Sinclair.

Chant skimmed the rest of the letter, which went on to reveal everything R. Edgar Blake knew—but, fortunately, not everything Martha Greenblatt knew—about him, apparently in order to establish the credibility of the writer. The signature at the bottom was a fairly good forgery of the woman's handwriting.

Chant crumpled up the letter and tossed it aside. He assumed copies had been hand-delivered by messenger to the New York offices of the FBI, NYPD, CIA, and possibly Interpol. Very soon, if it were not happening already, New York City would be swarming with people from many different agencies and countries, all looking for him. Also very soon, someone would come upon the carnage in the lecture hall at Blake College; the police would connect the murders with the letter, and might even now be on the way to the brownstone. . . .

Chant picked up the telephone on the writing desk and once again dialed Jan Rawlings's number. This time he let the phone ring twenty times before hanging up. He had not expected the phone to be answered, for he knew that the social worker was almost certainly dead by now. Hammerhead had done his homework before serving up his surprise in the lecture hall, Chant thought, and had gotten Jan Rawlings's name from his application, Martha's from a referral form Montsero had apparently requested. Now Tommy Wing was killing anyone he suspected might have suspicions about the experimental program.

At the very least, Chant thought, Hammerhead was using the murders, and Chant himself, to make certain the waters would be muddied for some time to come; there would be plenty of time for Blake to help Hammerhead disappear— and, perhaps, eclipse forever the real purpose of the experiments.

There was a Rolodex file on Martha's writing desk, and on impulse Chant spun it to the *R*s, flipped through the cards. There was a card for Jan Rawlings, listing both her home phone and a private office line. Chant again picked up the telephone, dialed the office number.

The line was busy; despite the lateness of the hour, someone was still in the large, communal office—and speaking on Jan Rawlings's private line.

In the distance he heard sirens, approaching and converging on the area from three different directions.

He would certainly not be safe on the streets in a stolen car, Chant thought. On foot, in the New York City night, it would be easy to elude capture by melting into the darkness—but that would not be the fastest way to get to Jan Rawlings's office building, which was where he had to go. As long as there was a chance she was still alive, he had to make every effort to make certain she stayed that way; since he could not reach her on the telephone, he would have to go to her.

The car he had come in could well have been reported stolen by now, Chant thought, which meant he needed other transportation. Martha's purse was on her dresser, and Chant quickly searched through it until he found the keys to her Mercedes. He went downstairs, through the kitchen and into the attached garage where the silver Mercedes was parked. Chant slid behind the wheel, started the engine, pushed the garage door opener, and pulled out onto the street.

Heading downtown, Chant stopped the car at the curb beside the first phone booth he came to. He dropped a quarter in the slot and again dialed Jan Rawlings's office number. The line was still busy. He got back in the Mercedes and started up.

He knew he was risking a great deal in what could turn out to be a futile gesture; by now the police would be searching hard for him, they would have his description, and there was a better than even chance they knew he was driving Martha's car. Someone else—a cleaning lady—could be using the social worker's phone, Chant thought, or she might simply have left it off the hook by accident before leaving the office. Still, he considered his course of action to be clear—and the car *was* the fastest way to get to the office building that loomed in the shadows of the great twin towers of the World Trade Center.

He turned south on the West Side Highway bypass, accelerated past the piers of the shipping lines that jutted into the Hudson River. As he stopped behind a car that had braked for a red light, two police cars with flashing lights pulled up on either side of him. The driver of the car to his left was talking excitedly into his radio, while his partner had drawn a gun and was shining a powerful flashlight into Chant's face; before the light blinded him, Chant had seen in the policeman's eyes a shock of recognition.

Chant jammed the gears into reverse, slammed the accelerator to the floorboards and popped the clutch. The engine and tires screamed as the car catapulted backward and caromed off the police car to Chant's right. The officer with the drawn gun leaned out the window and squeezed off a shot that shattered the Mercedes's windshield and whistled past Chant's ear.

Chant knew exactly where he wanted to go. He half turned in his seat and feathered the steering wheel slightly to his right. The rear of the car fishtailed, then veered sharply right. He lined up on his target, straightened the wheel and gripped it tightly to keep it in place. He crashed through a metal barrier and knocked over a fire hydrant before hitting the curb with a jolt that blew out both rear tires. Still he kept the accelerator to the floor as the car shot across the sidewalk and out a narrow loading dock toward the black, icy water of the Hudson.

CHAPTER ELEVEN ―――――

JAN SAT IN stunned disbelief, listening in amazement to the special news bulletin that had interrupted the Schubert symphony she'd been listening to. When the report was finished, Jan reached out with a trembling hand and shut off the small portable radio. Still numb with shock, she piled the client folders she had been updating into a neat, foot-high stack on the corner of her desk and replaced the telephone receiver in its cradle. Then she rose and went to the windows where she could see out over the Hudson River and the West Side of Manhattan. From her position on the seventeenth floor of the office building, she could clearly see the revolving, flashing red and white lights of at least half a dozen police cars parked at various angles around the pier where the man Martha Greenblatt had introduced to her as Neil Alter, driving Martha's stolen car, had reportedly plunged to his death in the ice-clogged river.

Jan understood none of it. Over the years she had read a number of articles about the infamous John Sinclair, renegade

American Army deserter and globe-trotting vigilante-mercenary-terrorist, but she could not understand how Martha Greenblatt—Jan was now certain that she had known Neil Alter's real identity—could have become involved with him.

Nor could Jan connect the gentle-eyed, gentle-voiced man who had twice met with her in this very office to an international criminal who had done all the terrible things reported in the media. In fact, for weeks Jan had been thinking a great deal about Neil Alter—who turned out to be John Sinclair, object of a twenty-year-long international manhunt.

Jan shuddered and wrapped her arms around her chest as she stared at the flashing lights. She remembered the feelings the man had stirred in her, recalled the night she had dreamed of him and awoke touching herself, straining against her cupped hand and probing fingers. Ah yes, Jan thought with a thin, wry smile. What a charmingly innocent, Bible Belt Baptist she was; the only man whose fantasy-form had driven her to masturbation and caused her to experience her first orgasm turned out to be a cunning criminal who had killed a countless number of people.

She started when she heard a noise behind her, wheeled around and saw a man standing in the doorway across the large room. The man appeared to be in his mid-fifties, with long, greasy gray hair that fell in pasty bands across his broad shoulders. His eyes were glassy, and the muscles in his face were slack, causing his jaw to droop slightly. His right hand was hidden inside the folds of a bulky wool overcoat.

Jan swallowed hard as she struggled to resist the panic that threatened to paralyze her. She drew herself up to her full height, cleared her throat, and forced herself to speak in a clear, strong voice. "I'm sorry, sir, but the office is closed now. There's no one here to help you. The security guard downstairs should have told you that."

The man gave no indication that he had heard her—or, if he had, cared. He abruptly began walking across the room toward Jan. Jan snatched up the telephone and, without taking her eyes off the man, started to dial the emergency police number.

The man's hand came out of the overcoat; he was holding a machete with a black bone handle and a long, curved blade that shone dully in the fluorescent light. The blade described an arc, and Jan pulled her hand away just in time to avoid having it cut off. The blade severed the telephone cord and buried itself in the wood. The man wriggled the blade back and forth to free it from the desktop while Jan trembled with terror. Her initial fear had been that the man with the vacant, glassy eyes and long, greasy hair meant to rape her; now she had the horrible realization that he had not come to rape or rob, only to kill.

The man's attack had come so quickly that Jan had not even had time to scream—and now she knew she was not going to. Screaming, she thought, was useless, since there was no one to hear her. Her only hope for survival lay in stealth and cunning.

She gripped her purse by its long, leather strap and swung it at the man's head. The blade flashed, and Jan was left holding on to a length of strap while the heavy leather bag flew through the air across the room, bounced off one of the other desks, and landed on the floor. Jan grabbed a wooden-handled letter opener from her desktop and brandished it, then realized how futile such a weapon was against a man wielding a machete.

She had to find a place to hide, Jan thought. The man was between her and the door, and she knew she could not hope to outrun him; with the lights on, it was only a matter of time before he trapped her and began chopping. There was only one place she could hide, and that was in the large, darkened conference room up the narrow stairs just behind and to her left.

The man was climbing up over the desk now, swinging the blade like a deadly metronome back and forth in front of her face. Jan kicked off her shoes, turned and ran up the stairs into

the darkness above. She heard the man stumble, then start to
come after her, his tread heavy on the stairs. Jan hurled herself
under a long, heavy conference table, crawled to the other
side and cringed behind one of the wide table legs.

After a few moments Jan screwed up her courage, rose to
her knees, and peered over the top of the table. She could see
the man's figure silhouetted in the doorway against the light
from the office below; he was searching for the light switch.
He found it, and a second later the lights came on.

Jan ducked, spun around and jammed the point of the letter
opener into the wall socket behind her. Sparks and blue flame
danced across the metal blade of the opener, but the wood
handle protected Jan and the room went dark.

The man hesitated just a moment, then began walking
around the table. He was dragging the machete blade across
the wood surface, and the odd, silky sound of steel sliding
across the polished tabletop sent chills through Jan. The man
bumped into a chair and, still without speaking a word, began
mechanically hacking at it. Jan used the sound to cover her
movements; she crawled on her hands and knees back under
the table, made her way to the far corner of the room, and
huddled in a corner.

Having demolished the chair, the man continued his circuit
around the table. He paused twenty feet away from Jan, man
and poised machete outlined by the moonlight streaming in
through the windows at the far end of the room.

Suddenly there was a soft but distinct popping sound, like
the snapping of someone's fingers. The sound came from
somewhere in the darkness along the wall to Jan's left, just
inside the doorway. The man with the machete tensed, cocked
his head in that direction. The sound was repeated, this time
slightly louder. The man in the moonlight raised his blade,
lurched in the direction of the sound, and disappeared into the
darkness amid the sound of crashing chairs. Jan cringed at the
thwack-thwack of steel striking wood.

To Jan's astonishment, another, different silhouette suddenly glided into the wide pool of moonlight, moving silent as

a shadow. It was the silhouette of a tall man, well over six feet, and his shirt hung in shreds about his chest and shoulders. There was something familiar about the movements and shape of the silhouetted figure, and Jan had to jam her knuckles into her mouth to keep from crying out in shock—and joy.

The tall man raised his right arm and snapped his fingers, once.

Suddenly the man with the machete came hurtling out of the darkness, machete held high with both hands over his head. He brought the blade slicing down toward the top of the other figure's head, but by then the tall man was no longer there. Moving with the speed and grace of a ballet dancer, Chant moved easily to one side as the blade sliced down through the empty space where he had been standing only a moment before. A knee shot up into the killer's stomach, and for the first time a sound issued from the man's throat as he doubled over and gasped for air. The machete clattered to the floor as Chant's hand came down on the back of the killer's neck. There was a cracking sound, and the killer collapsed to the floor.

Somehow, Jan knew her attacker had died almost instantly. It seemed to her that everything had happened in the space of a single breath.

"Holy shit," Jan heard herself say.

"Are you all right, Miss Rawlings?" Chant asked as he turned the killer over in a pool of moonlight and began to search through his pockets.

Jan's response was to giggle. She felt weightless, turned inside out, floating somewhere inside the shell of her own body. "I am certainly *not* all right!" she managed to blurt between bursts of hysterical laughter. "As any one of my clients might put it, I'm scared out of my fucking gourd!"

Chant stopped what he was doing and looked in her direction. "Are you hurt?"

Jan brought her hysteria under control. She clenched her fists, took a deep breath, got to her feet, and walked into the moonlight. "No," she said evenly. "Thanks to you, I'm not hurt."

"Good," Chant replied perfunctorily as he went back to searching through the dead man's clothing.

Jan studied the man with the iron-colored hair and eyes. "You . . . uh, you're . . . ?"

"I am."

"The radio . . ."

"Never believe everything you hear on the radio or read in the newspapers."

"Uh . . . wow. First impressions can be notoriously misleading, of course, but I liked you the first time I saw you, and I like you even better right now. I must have a thing for big-time crooks."

Chant looked up at the woman, laughed easily. "It'll pass, Miss Rawlings. I'm sure of it."

Suddenly Jan's legs would no longer support her, and she sat down hard on the floor. Chant started to rise and go to her, but Jan shook her head to signal she was all right. Chant returned to his search, and Jan watched as he turned out the man's empty pockets, then ripped open the coat and shirt collar. The labels in the man's clothing had all been removed.

"I don't understand," Jan said in a small voice. "The security guard downstairs . . . ?"

"He's dead."

"Oh," Jan swallowed hard, trying to raise some moisture in her dry mouth. "You're supposed to be dead, too."

'Yeah. Well, remember what you said about first impressions."

"He killed the Greenblatts, didn't he?"

"Maybe; I'm not sure. This isn't the man I expected would come after you."

"Not the man you *expected*?!"

Chant did not reply. He rose, walked to the window, and stared out over the city, apparently lost in thought.

"Mr. Alt—Sinclair?" Jan continued tentatively. "I don't suppose you'd care to explain to me what's going on?"

Chant turned around and stared at Jan for a few moments, then shook his head. "No. I'm sorry, Miss Rawlings, but I don't have time. Con Ed will have noticed the power surge when you short-circuited the lights, and they may send a man to investigate. I can't be here."

"*Why?* You can explain it to them, and then—"

"It's a long story, Miss Rawlings, and explaining it to anyone isn't important. What's important is the fact that you're alive. Now we want to make certain that you stay alive."

"*What?* Good grief! You mean—?"

"I don't want to frighten you, Miss Rawlings, but you could be in danger for . . . some time; until a stop is put to this thing." Chant paused, groaned as he arched his back. "Move out of your apartment for a time; stay with a friend. Try not to be alone at all, but especially never work alone at night here again."

Jan had seen the grimace on his face when he'd arched his back; now she thought she detected strain in his voice. "*You're* hurt," she said softly.

"Not really. Just a few scrapes and bruises."

Jan walked to him, turned him around so that she could see his back in the moonlight, winced. "My God, it's raw."

"It's not as bad as it probably looks."

"How the hell do you know?" Jan said, still wincing at the sight of the raw, bleeding flesh on Chant's back. "You can't see it."

"It will heal."

"The car—you jumped out before it went in the water."

Chant nodded, turned back to Jan.

"But how did you get away from the police? How did you get here?"

Chant shrugged, smiled thinly. "The dock pilings; while they were looking for me in the water, I moved back along the struts under the dock and came up behind them."

"If it weren't for you, I'd be dead. I owe you my life."

"You don't owe me anything; I owed you. I allowed a lovely friend with a silver tongue—Martha—to talk me into doing something I was initially against. It cost her her life. If this man had killed you, I'd also be responsible for your death."

"You know, I don't have the slightest idea what you're talking about."

"I let her refer me to you."

"That still doesn't explain anything. Why did you want to be referred to me?"

"I needed a way to get into the project over at Blake College."

"Why?"

"I must go now, Miss Rawlings," Chant said, heading for the door. "Call the police, tell them exactly what happened here."

"But then they'll start looking for you again!"

"It can't be helped, and it really doesn't matter," Chant said, pausing in the doorway. "I don't think the people who sent this man after you will try again—too risky. Still, you must be cautious. Take the steps I recommended."

"Wait a minute!" Jan cried, running after Chant as he disappeared down the stairs. She made it down the stairs and across the office in time to block the door. Suddenly she was very angry—without understanding why. She felt as if this man standing before her with a bemused smile on his face was taking something away from her, something irreplaceable which she had only just begun to realize she had.

"I do have to go," Chant said gently.

"Mr. Sinclair," Jan said in what she hoped was a light manner, "this may come as a shock to you, but I'm absolutely *petrified* right now. Can't you just stay with me for a little while?"

"You'll be all right, Miss Rawlings, if you do what I told you to do. Go back and call the police. There's no one else coming after you, and the police will be here in a few minutes—if they're not on the way already. It's why I must leave."

"Let me come with you!"

Chant gently pushed Jan out of the doorway. "Good-bye, Miss Rawlings."

She had lied, Jan thought as she watched the man with the iron-colored eyes and hair walk out of the office and disappear around a corner. She was not afraid; in fact, she was excited by the sudden conviction that John Sinclair was a gift sent to her by . . . whatever. He was a gift that could either crush her or transform her into a person she had never dreamed she could be. He was leaving; whatever she did now, or did not do, would affect her powerfully until the day she died. And the decision had to be made immediately, for the gift would never be offered to her again. With John Sinclair gone, she would be left with nothing but memories of a man who was like some primitive, inexorable force—left with nothing but a sense of mystery that would never be solved, and could only hurt.

Jan grabbed her shoes and purse. Then, still in her stocking feet, she ran out of the office and turned down the corridor to her left. She caught sight of Chant just as he was stepping into an elevator, and suddenly tears welled in her eyes and she had to choke back a sob; away from her eyes, Chant's body was sagging with exhaustion and knotted with pain. This man had just saved her life, Jan thought, and now he needed help. She intended to make certain he got it.

"Wait, Mr. Sinclair!" Jan shouted, frantically waving a shoe as the elevator door started to close. "Damn it, I'm afraid! You got me into this! Whether you like it or not, I'm sticking with you until you get me out of it!"

CHAPTER TWELVE _____

UNABLE TO SLEEP, Jan arose just after dawn and tiptoed down the steps from her bedroom on the second floor so as not to awaken the man she assumed was still sleeping. The delicious aroma of brewing tea was her first clue that Chant was already awake, and she found him sitting at the kitchen table. Dressed in jeans, sneakers, and a sweatshirt Jan presumed had come from one of the two bulky suitcases he had retrieved from somewhere in Central Park the night before, he was reading a small, leather-bound book, gently turning yellowed pages so old that the printing had faded—another treasure, she thought, from the disinterred suitcases.

"Good morning," Chant said easily, closing the ancient book and carefully setting it aside. "How are you feeling?"

"How am I feeling? How are *you* feeling? Good grief, you must have some recuperative powers!"

"I told you my back probably looked worse than it was. It's still a bit tender, but you did a marvelous job of washing and bandaging. Also, the ointment is very effective." .

"God, what was in that stuff?" Jan asked, wrinkling her nose as she remembered the smell of the black, greasy salve Chant had given her to rub into the wounds on his back.

"Just an herbal concoction I was taught to make some years ago. I'd give you the recipe, but you can't find the ingredients in this country. I always carry some with me."

"Along with disguises, false passports, and wads of cash in six different currencies—which you keep in suitcases you've hidden somewhere."

Chant laughed easily. "Doesn't everyone?"

"I've been listening to the radio most of the night. You should hear some of the crazy things they're saying."

"I've probably already heard most of them—a number of times."

"The reports say that some people call you 'Chant,' but nobody seems to know why," Jan said, once again marveling at the big man's grace of movement as he rose, poured her a cup of tea, brought it to her.

"It's just a nickname," Chant replied, pouring himself a second cup, sitting back down at the table across from Jan.

"How did you get it?"

"It's just a nickname."

"Meaning you won't tell me."

"Meaning it's not important."

"I like it. May I call you Chant?"

"If you'd like."

"This is the best tea I've ever tasted," Jan said, sipping at the steaming brew. "From the suitcases?"

Chant smiled, nodded. "There are some amenities I prefer not to do without."

Jan set down her cup, leaned across the table, and touched Chant's hand. "Thank you again for saving my life last night."

"I told you there was nothing to thank me for," Chant replied evenly. "Now I'm the one who's indebted to you. Looking the way I did last night, I think I might have had a little trouble getting a cab, not to mention a hotel room. And look where I ended up—a lovely house, surrounded by trees, in Rockland County."

Jan shrugged. "No big deal. It's just a good thing for both of us that you happened to save my life on a Friday night. I always come up here on weekends, so I'd already rented a car. I was coming anyway; the only difference is that now I have some interesting company."

"Your house?"

Jan shook her head. "Social workers can't afford homes on South Mountain Road; this is serious movie star country. The deal is a legacy from a rich ex-boyfriend. We somehow managed to stay friends even after we broke up. He just sees it as a summer house; he can't be bothered to come up here during the winter, but it's also a bother to shut a house down. We have an arrangement where I use it on weekends in exchange for watering the plants, making sure the pipes haven't frozen, that sort of thing. Being able to come out here is about the only thing that allows me to keep my sanity." Jan paused, added quietly: "Can we talk now? Will you explain to me what's happening?"

Occasionally sipping at his tea, Chant began to talk about Vito Biaggi and the Italian magistrate's investigation. He told Jan about his friend's murder, and the slaying of a diplomat in Switzerland in a similar fashion. He told her everything, in detail, up to the moment when he had slipped into the darkened conference room and intercepted her attacker, for he knew there was no longer any point in concealing anything from the woman.

Through it all, Jan listened in wide-eyed silence. "My God," she said when he had finished. "You were certainly right on target when you suspected something strange might be going on in that research project." She wanted to say more, but simply ended by reaching out and again touching his hand. She felt short of breath in the presence of this man whose firm, even tone when he had spoken of the deaths of Vito Biaggi and Martha Greenblatt belied the deep sorrow and regret she felt radiating from him like fever heat. John Sinclair, she thought, was not a man who wasted extra words or emotion.

"Yes, but what I didn't anticipate was that I'd be recognized—in this case, by an old enemy. Once the people behind the project realized that it had been penetrated, they felt the need not only to dismantle it, but to kill anyone with whom I might have conceivably shared information about it.

"I was left alive as a smoke screen and in order to have someone on whom to blame the murders. They were certain no one would believe any story I had to tell; because of my reputation in some quarters, my guilt would automatically be assumed. It's the same principle that was at work in the other two assassinations—and I suspect there may have been even more. I should have found a way of getting into the program without using Martha to deceive you."

"I don't know any other way you could have done it," Jan said quietly.

"I should have found a way."

"Chant, what is it that these people were doing?"

"The whole focus of the project was to select the most vicious and physically fit of the ex-convicts who were fed into it; over the years, I believe these men were—are—meant to be used as assassins. But not in the usual sense."

"What do you mean?"

"Did you notice anything unusual about the man who attacked you?"

Jan laughed nervously. "I can't say I paid much attention to anything but the machete in his hands."

"Did you see his face at all?"

"He had just this dull expression—blank, really; he didn't show any emotion at all. He was like a machine that just kept coming at me—until you arrived on the scene."

"Right; 'like a machine' seems an apt description. The men I've been with were many things, but they certainly weren't unemotional, they weren't suicidal, and the worst of them wouldn't take it into his head to hack up a stranger for no reason. I believe that man was somehow programmed to kill you; I believe he may have been sent to your apartment first, then picked up and brought to the office building when you didn't come home. He seemed to be in a kind of trance, incapable of any real decision. If I'm right—and I'm certain I am—he was a 'graduate' of that program at Blake College, a man who'd made it through to the end."

Jan shook her head. "But where's he been all this time?"

"A good question. Just before I had my rather unpleasant reunion with Tommy Wing, Montsero was saying that he had a proposition for us. I think I know what that proposition was—a quick, secret move away from New York to a place where they'd have secure, well-paying jobs and new identities. That was the 'reward' for completing the program. Wherever they ended up, they'd be added to a stockpile of manpower to be used as kind of throwaway assassins, human bullets which are totally expendable, and which may even be programmed to kill themselves if they're not killed by police. The first thing we do now is look for the place where they may be keeping this human ammunition dump."

Jan smiled. "I like the fact that you said 'we.' I take it as a hopeful sign you're not as anxious to get rid of me now as you were last night."

Chant studied Jan for some time in silence. "Things are different now, Jan," he said at last. "Last night, if you'd stayed and reported what happened to the police, I think the people who've done these things would have taken the calculated risk of ignoring you. By now, they know you're with me and that you know everything I know. Now they can't ignore you. They'll be hunting you every bit as intently as they're hunting me. I really don't want you killed. Considering the power and resources of these people, I consider you as safe— probably safer—with me as you would be anywhere else. Until this is resolved, you can never go back to places you've been or contact people you've known."

"Oh," Jan said in a small voice, and wondered why she wasn't upset in the least at leaving everything in her past life behind her. "Where will we start looking?"

"In the library. We'll be going through a lot of back issues of business magazines."

"What will we be looking for?"

"The founder of Blake College is a man by the name of R. Edgar Blake." Chant paused, smiled thinly. "Another old enemy. Knowing Blake, I'd guess that the college was founded precisely for the purpose of running that project; he's not much of a philanthropist. If Blake is behind the project, it probably means he uses—or controls the use—of these throwaway assassins. Attacking Blake is also going to present some special problems, since he's probably the most well-guarded man in the world. What we'll be looking for is a place—some kind of holding that can be linked to Blake—where he might be keeping these men."

"Chant, if what you say is true, then it's this Blake who's ultimately responsible for the deaths of Martha and your friend in Italy."

"Yes. It makes Blake part of the organization Vito was after—probably the head."

"And this Tommy Wing is his chief of security?"

Chant shook his head. "Not likely."

"But—?"

"Tommy Wing isn't exactly what you'd call a good soldier or organizational type. Blake obviously gives him little chores to do, but my guess is that Blake keeps him around as a kind of pet."

"A kind of *pet!*"

Chant shrugged, smiled. "I'm quite serious. Some people keep dogs, cats, goldfish, or snakes around as pets; Blake would keep a Tommy Wing. For Blake, evil is a kind of hobby; it would amuse him to keep on his payroll a man who bites other men to death. Also, if you *really* wanted to put a scare into somebody, Hammerhead would be the man to do it. It's not the same thing as security, which requires professionals. R. Edgar Blake has the best-equipped and best-trained private army on the face of the earth. Anyway, I know some of his holdings in this country, and I'm hoping the business magazines will help us to pinpoint some others; it won't be easy, because he controls holding companies within holding companies. We'll focus on Texas."

"Why Texas?"

"A man by the name of Ron Press disappeared shortly after going through the program. He wrote one letter to his girl-friend after that, mentioning that he'd landed a good job. The letter came from somewhere in Texas. It's the only lead I have. Knowing where to *find* Blake isn't a problem; but I want to destroy this operation, and doing so may give me some idea of how to get to him."

"Chant, who *is* this R. Edgar Blake? I've never heard of him."

"You're not supposed to have heard of him; he spends a lot of time and money keeping his name out of the newspapers. But he's arguably the richest man in the world—he at least ranks in the top five, along with a few members of the Saudi royal family. He's also among the most powerful men in the world. He lives as a recluse in a castle overlooking Lake Geneva, in Switzerland, but his influence reaches around the globe. He's a peculiarly evil man—evil and peculiar in the sense that he doesn't *have* to corrupt or kill to keep his wealth growing and his power intact; he simply enjoys it."

"The kind of man who'd keep this Hammerhead as a kind of pet."

"Ah; now you're getting a good picture of R. Edgar. Crushing or twisting other people's lives out of shape is apparently what keeps his juices going. He has to be pushing eighty. Also, he has a pretty good hate on for me, and I'm sure that keeps him hopping around his castle."

"Why does he hate you?"

Chant smiled. "I once stole two million dollars from him."

Jan laughed. "That sounds like a pretty good reason."

"Actually, two million dollars is like pocket change to

Blake. But Blake is used to stealing money from other people; he doesn't like people stealing it from him. It's a matter of principle."

"How did you steal it from him?"

"One of thousands of little companies he owns manufactures powdered milk, in this country. Something went wrong with the equipment. It wasn't detected right away, and for a week or so the company was running batches of contaminated product. The problem was discovered by one of the company's chemists, and the executives dutifully notified the FDA. The bad product was recalled from around the country, the equipment was fixed and inspected, and business went on as usual. It resulted in the loss of a few million dollars, but in terms of the overall worth and revenues of the company it was nothing more than a quarterly writeoff on taxes. Well, somehow R. Edgar got wind of what had happened, and decided that a tax writeoff wasn't enough. He fired the chemist, who happens to be a friend of mine, and all the management, then put in other people who proceeded to make arrangements for selling the contaminated product to various third-world countries. Actually, what they were doing was perfectly legal—but it meant that the bad batches were going to wind up in the stomachs of a lot of children who were already sick or starving.

"I arranged to set myself up as a commodities exchange dealer for that bit of business. R. Edgar's powdered milk disappeared into thin air, and I managed to relieve him of two million dollars in the process. It was really a very simple operation, but I happen to know that he's spent more than two million just paying men to search for me. I don't mind that. But in the process, he's also managed to find out a good deal about me; that I do mind."

"I'll bet he even knows why they call you 'Chant.'"

Jan's words had been delivered in a light, coquettish tone; Chant's reply was deadly serious. "He may. In any case, his men can stop looking for me. I'm going to destroy his operation, and then I'm going to kill him."

Jan stared at the man with the iron-colored eyes some time before speaking again. "It doesn't bother you at all that so many men are hunting you, does it?" she asked quietly.

Chant's features softened, and he laughed. "Bother me? Of course, it bothers me. Sometimes—like last night, for example—it can be a major distraction."

Jan didn't smile. "But you're not afraid."

"I've been hunted for many years, Jan," Chant said seriously, "by many different men and organizations, for many different reasons. I look on it as a cost of doing business."

"Business?"

"Trying to relieve men like R. Edgar Blake of some of their hard-earned money is what I do for a living, Jan." Chant paused, smiled thinly. "I thought you'd read about me."

Jan shook her head slightly. "What I've read and heard isn't what you're all about at all, John Sinclair. From the first time I saw you, I knew you were a good and gentle man, a man who could be trusted." Now Jan paused, brushed her silky blonde hair back from her face. "But you don't really need anybody's help, do you?"

"I don't understand what you're really asking or saying," Chant replied quietly.

"I mean, here you are in an area filled with men hunting you, and you blithely continue to plan your own hunt. Talk about cool!"

"I told you it's my business, Jan. The key to success always lies in the gathering of sufficient information and proper planning for an operation, which can take months. In this instance I stumbled into something blindly, without proper intelligence or time to prepare. My carelessness cost a friend and her husband their lives, as well as the life of a man who believed the lies I told him. I must do what I can to make up for these things."

Jan cocked her head, studied the man sitting across from her. "You operate just like the general everyone said you'd be before you walked away from the war; except now you're your own one-man army."

"I'm afraid the war is something I don't discuss," Chant said evenly.

"There are a lot of things you don't discuss, but that's fine with me. Chant, will you make love to me?"

Chant raised his eyebrows slightly. "Not if it's because you're thinking that's a way to repay me for saving your life."

Jan shook her head. "That isn't the reason."

"You're trembling. Are you still afraid?"

"No; I'm not afraid because I'm with you. But I am troubled about something which *I* don't care to talk about—at least not at the moment. I'm not trying to meet your needs, only my own. Will you make love to me? It would make a lovely morning even lovelier."

Chant, who had been studying the woman closely while she spoke, said quietly, "Those words were extremely difficult for you, weren't they?"

"Yes," Jan murmured, lowering her gaze. "I've never asked a man to make love to me before. The problem is . . . I've never *wanted* a man to make love to me before." She paused, laughed nervously. "What a bigmouth I am! I said I didn't want to talk about it, and there I just went ahead and talked about it."

Chant rose, walked around the table, and gently wrapped her in his arms.

CHAPTER THIRTEEN ⸻

CHANT LEANED BACK in his chair in the study carrel, rubbed his eyes, then reached out and shut off the computer terminal. Working from what knowledge he had of R. Edgar Blake's holdings, he had rapidly scanned the indexes of dozens of back issues of *Fortune, Business Week,* and a number of foreign business journals looking for more leads. He had come up empty. If R. Edgar Blake had holdings in Texas, Chant thought, it was going to take a considerable number of hours to find out what they were.

He sensed Jan come up behind him, felt her gently touch his shoulder. "I have something here I think may interest you, mysterious sir," the woman said, her voice rich with pride and happiness. "Your friend Blake may not like to see his name in the newspapers, but he doesn't seem to mind putting it—or, in this case, his initials—on things he owns."

Jan reached over Chant's shoulder, placed a photocopy of an article in the carrel. Chant scanned the article, then turned in his chair, smiled at Jan, and gave her a thumbs-up sign.

"What do you think?" Jan continued, grinning broadly. "Am I earning my keep?"

"I think you look great as a redhead in horn-rimmed glasses." Chant folded the paper and put it in his pocket, then rose and led Jan by the arm toward the exit of the Forty-Second Street Library. "I also think you've earned yourself a first-class meal, and I believe I know just the restaurant."

"Very fine work, Jan," Chant said quietly as the waiter at the French restaurant took their order and departed. "I couldn't find anything in the places I was looking. What made you think of looking in medical journals?"

"I thought you weren't supposed to talk about anything important in public places," Jan whispered.

"Our table is far enough away from the others for us to speak freely, as long as we keep our voices low—and I'm glad to see how sensitive you are to the problem. Just don't ever slip and call me 'Chant' in public."

Jan nodded. "Are you *ever* going to tell me how you got that nickname?"

"It's a long story, Jan."

"It probably has to do with things you did in the war, which means you'll never tell me," Jan said, drawing the corners of her mouth down in a playful pout.

"I may," Chant replied evenly. "But not now."

"Fair enough," Jan said, and smiled. "As to your question, I knew you were trying to track this Blake through business publications, so I didn't think it made much sense for me to duplicate your efforts. I remembered the blank look on that man's face, and your comment that you thought he and others like him were probably programmed in some way; so I told the librarian I was interested in medical or pharmaceutical journals dealing specifically with hypnotic and psychotropic drugs, and she helped me find them. I found that piece in the third pharmaceutical journal I looked in—gluteathin, GTN, which is the most powerful of the new hypnotic drugs; it's strictly controlled, and currently used only in a few licensed psychiatric research centers. There were a few other candidates for a drug that could induce a trance and make the subject highly suggestible, but GTN was the only one licensed for manufacture in only one place in the world—R.E.B. Pharmaceuticals, in Houston, Texas."

"My dear, why don't you pick out the most expensive wine on that list?"

"I can't drink worth a damn, and you're the only intoxicant I need. Will we go to Houston now?"

"I'll be going to Houston, Jan," Chant said gently. "But not for a week or so. There's other information I want to get on Blake and R.E.B. Pharmaceuticals, and New York libraries are the best place to do the research. Thanks to you, I know now where to look."

"But I won't be going with you to Houston?" Jan asked carefully.

"No, Jan."

"I thought you said—"

"It would be a needless risk for you to travel with me to Houston. I'm sending you to England for a while."

"England?"

"Arrangements will be made to get you a false passport, and somebody who works for me in England will come to escort you back with him. When you meet him, you'll use the code words, 'Cooked Goose.' The man's name is Alistair."

"'Cooked Goose'? What on earth does that mean?"

"They're just code words. It will assure Alistair that you come from me and can be completely trusted; he'll know he won't have to be guarded with you."

"You won't be with me when I meet this man?"

"Probably not. Alistair's a rather elderly gentleman, so traveling with him will be a good disguise in addition to the one you're wearing. He's a very good man, and he'll take good care of you."

"Will I ever see you again?"

"A hard question to answer at this point, Jan. The most important thing is that I'll know you'll be safe until this thing is over."

Or until he was dead, Chant thought. Either way, he knew Alistair would do everything in his power, even give his life, to keep the woman from harm. And his English estate was certainly safer than the streets of Houston.

"I haven't been useful to you?"

Chant smiled. "You've been invaluable."

"Then—"

She stopped speaking when Chant abruptly put a finger to his lips, and a moment later a waiter appeared at the table with their appetizers. Jan was thankful for the interruption, for she had been about to blurt out things that would have made her seem foolish—and perhaps have pushed John Sinclair away from her forever. She ate the appetizer and the rest of her meal in silence, which the man sitting across from her seemed content not to break. When the coffee was served, she stirred in a single spoonful of sugar, sipped at the dark, rich brew, then looked up at Chant.

"Last night was wonderful, John," she said in a voice she was gratified to find did not tremble. "You're an incredible lover. I was afraid I was frigid; now I know I'm not."

"That's an understatement, if ever I've heard one."

"Thank you."

"Thank *you*."

Jan shook her head slightly. "There's no way for you to understand and appreciate how much I have to thank you for. Two and a half years ago I tried to kill myself."

Jan paused, searching Chant's face anxiously for signs of shock, pity, or embarrassment, but found in his eyes only concern and compassion.

"Now I look upon what I did as an act of stupidity, self-pity, and cowardice," Jan continued in a voice just above a whisper. "But at the time . . . I didn't know how else to deal with despair and depression that just wouldn't go away. I didn't seem to be able to love like other people, and I certainly didn't find any satisfaction in sex; sex was just something that disgusted me. My career was a devastating disappointment; when you saw me on Christmas Eve, you found me in one of my *better* moods. I took my degree in social work because I so badly wanted to help people who needed it. You can say I was naive, but I truly believed I could change a little piece of the world. Well, I quickly found out I couldn't; there are so *many* people who need help, who just can't cope, and I ended up just pushing papers at them. I have—had—a caseload of almost a hundred people, which made it impossible for me to really do anything for any of them. I felt so *useless*. I still wanted so badly to help, to make a *difference*, but I knew I never would. I figured I was going to have to spend the rest of my life feeling like . . . like . . .

"Then a man by the name of Neil Alter came along, and I found myself terribly attracted to him—or maybe to some quality in him, if it's not the same thing. Then all of *this* happened. Neil Alter turned out to be someone else entirely, and this someone else brought meaning and excitement into my life and made me *want* to live again.

"And then I did something incredibly selfish; I demanded that this man take me along with him, to personally protect me. I lied to you, John. I wasn't afraid of being killed; I was afraid that an opportunity to escape from what I felt was a useless life was slipping away. Suddenly, you were my lifeline. I wanted to go with you because it gave me an excuse to turn my back on everything I had come to loathe.

"I'm not a giddy schoolgirl, John—even if I sound like one at times. I'm not saying I love you, and I certainly don't entertain any thought of you loving me. I'm just trying to be totally upfront with you now in the hope that maybe . . . I'm saying, I guess, that this experience is probably the best thing that ever happened to me; I've never felt so *alive* as I have the past two days.

"But that isn't the point. I'm not asking you to give me anything more than you've already given me, and I'm certainly not asking you to feel responsible for me. I'm saying that, no matter what happens, I won't be going back to the life I had; it wasn't a life. On the other hand, I think I've already proven that I *can* be useful to you. I'm smart, John, and I'd work hard for you. I know you have people working for you, like this Alistair you want me to go away with. Let *me* work for you, in whatever capacity. What *you* do has an impact. No matter what others say about you, you are an incredibly decent man who helps many people others can't, or won't, help. I think I'm a decent person, and I know I've always wanted to help. I understand that there's great danger in the things that you do, and that I could easily be killed one of these days. I take total responsibility for that."

"Would you like dessert?" Chant asked quietly.

"No," Jan said, raising her chin defiantly. "What I want is a job—with you. Let me stay with you. You can trust me; I won't betray you, ever."

"I know I can trust you," Chant said evenly as he signaled for the waiter.

Jan waited, head held high, while Chant paid the bill and got their coats. She had, Jan thought, made her case the best she could, and would say no more. She had lied about only one thing; she believed she *was* in love with John Sinclair.

"You have a job," Chant said at last as they walked back to the car Chant had rented with a credit card matched to his present false identity.

"Thank you, mysterious sir," Jan said, tears misting her eyes.

"Even if you wanted to, you couldn't go back to your old life until this is over, so I may as well put you on the payroll. But you're still going to England."

"Oh," Jan said, making no effort to hide her disappointment.

"I always work alone in the field, Jan; it has nothing to do with you. However, I still have to contact Alistair, and it will take at least two or three days for him to make the necessary arrangements. During that time, working only from libraries in Rockland County, I want you to see if you can find out anything about the R.E.B. complex itself—size, number of employees, range of products, anything at all. Information, Jan, is the most potent weapon. Since you like to think of me as a general, you may now think of yourself as my chief of intelligence-gathering. No detail is unimportant."

"I understand."

"In any writing or note-taking you do, make sure you never link your name with mine. It would be a good idea for you to construct a code to write your notes in—even better if you can commit what you learn to memory."

"I understand."

"It's very important, when you research for an operation, to understand the precise objectives of that operation. In Houston, my objective will be to penetrate the complex in order to gather written records, or some other kind of proof, of what's being done with these men. Also, to find—"

"I understand what you want to do there, Chant," Jan interrupted quietly. "I told you I'm smart."

"Don't be too quick to understand, Jan, and don't try to be too smart until you've been at this awhile. A single piece of information can mean the difference between life and death."

"Will you let me come back into New York to research? Out in Rockland, no single library will have all the resources I may need, and there's no time to use the interlibrary system."

"You have a point; I'll think about it. First, let's see what you find in the Rockland libraries."

"All right."

"Bear in mind that I'll be using the information you gather to formulate a plan to achieve those precise objectives I mentioned. In Houston, I want to get in and out without Blake learning that I've ever been there; but the assassin operation must be effectively destroyed, and I'd like to end with the names of any and all people who may have used them."

"Precisely what your friend was trying to do."

"Yes. The second operation is one you can research even if you're in England by the time you start working on it. You'll find out anything you can about that castle of Blake's on Lake

Geneva. It's probably the most secure complex on earth, but it's also centuries old, a historical site, so some architectural details may be available in various magazines. If you can find recent aerial photographs, that would be wonderful; if not, you and Alistair will arrange to have our own taken. Incidentally, until you've gotten the hang of all this, never contract for services with an outsider until you've checked with Alistair or me."

"What's your objective in Geneva?"

"Simply to kill Blake."

"And get away."

"That would be nice."

"Chant, please let me come to Houston with you. You can do your thing, and I'll do mine. I won't be in the way, I'll stay well away from any danger, and you'll have me right there to provide you with information as I find it. It will save you an awful lot of time."

Alistair Powers and Jan Rawlings were going to get along just fine, Chant thought. He said, "No. If you're going to work for me, you must learn to follow my instructions precisely."

"Yes, mysterious sir," Jan said, and sighed.

They rode in comfortable silence, Jan's head resting on Chant's shoulder, back up the Palisades Parkway to Rockland County and the house on South Mountain Road. They got out of the car, walked up a long, sloping path to the door. Jan opened it, stepped inside, reached for the lights—and suddenly felt Chant's strong grip on her wrist, pulling her hand away from the light switch. Then he shoved her gently but firmly back into the shadows in a corner of the foyer. With Chant standing in the moonlight streaming in through the open door, Jan was amazed to see a knife suddenly appear, as if materializing out of thin air, in his right hand. Then he darted quickly but in virtually complete silence up the stairs.

Jan waited, her heart pounding, in silent darkness that became almost a palpably heavy thing, pressing on her lungs.

Then the lights came on upstairs, and she heard Chant's voice.

"It's all right, Jan. You can come up."

Jan hurried up the stairs, found him in his bedroom. His knife had been returned to his sleeve, or wherever it had come from, but the expression on his face was intense as he slowly turned, studying everything in the room.

"Someone's been here?" Jan asked breathlessly.

Chant nodded, continued to slowly turn.

"But nothing's been disturbed."

"You're wrong. Everything in my room and yours—and probably in the house—has been gone through, by an expert."

Jan sniffed, suddenly aware of a faint medicinal odor in the room, like strong mouthwash. "What's that smell?"

"It belongs to the man who was in here," Chant replied in a low tone. "His name's Duane Insolers, and he works for R. Edgar Blake. He's a bright man, obviously good at what he does."

"But how could he have found us, Chant?!"

Chant shrugged. "Most likely, he posed as a police detective, talked to some of your friends and found out about this place. It doesn't matter how; he's been here."

"What now?"

"Get your coat, Jan. We've run out of time, and we're leaving right now."

Jan quickly went to her room. She put on her coat, made certain she erased the smile on her face before she turned to face Chant, who was standing in the doorway, coat on and suitcases in his hands.

"I'm ready, Chant."

"Listen to me carefully, Jan," Chant said in a flat voice. "Frankly, I'm surprised we're alive right now—but we are. There's no reason to assume Insolers knows we're aware that he's watching us, which gives us a certain element of surprise. I think I can—"

"There's no doubt whatsoever in my mind that you can do anything you say you can do—along with an almost infinite variety of things you don't say you can do."

"This isn't a game, Jan; you could end up with a bullet in your head very quickly. First, we'll use the balcony outside your bedroom to get up on the roof. Second, I want you to do exactly as I say, no matter how strange any instruction I give you may seem, immediately and without question. With a little luck, I think we should be able to get past whoever may be waiting for us outside, and be on our way."

"Got it."

"Take off your shoes and put one in each pocket of your coat. Also, begin right now to concentrate on breathing deeply and regularly; it will help you to relax and move quietly, and will also reduce the risk of hyperventilation if something startles you."

"Yes, sir," Jan said seriously—but she could not resist snapping a salute and adding, "Let's go, boss."

CHAPTER FOURTEEN _____

CHANT BROUGHT THE rented Cessna Executive in to a smooth landing at the small, private airport just outside Houston. He taxied to his designated parking area, but before getting out he carefully packed his array of rented photographic equipment back into a leather satchel; he did not want anyone at the airport to know he had been taking aerial photographs.

It had been a long day, and it was not yet over; he still had to drive to the photographic studio he had rented in order to develop the film he had shot. Long, Chant thought, but productive.

Up before dawn, he had spent the early morning hours driving his rented car on the highways and roads surrounding the R.E.B. Pharmaceuticals plant, stopping occasionally to study sections of the complex through binoculars or take photographs with the macrotelescopic lens on his Nikon. From the distance around the complex, Chant estimated that R.E.B. Pharmaceuticals occupied a tract of at least a hundred acres. There appeared to be three different sections to R.E.B. Phar-

maceuticals—a manufacturing complex, a warehousing and
shipping area, and a smaller area with windowless buildings
and a high-tech look, which Chant suspected comprised a
research-and-development facility. Each area had its own employee parking lots and entrance from access roads, with the
research area surrounded by warning signs and electrified
fences topped with barbed wire. There were uniformed guards
at each of the entrances, with a double contingent around the
research area.

Chant had been impressed by the appearance of the security personnel. They were, he thought, not the usual contingent of retired police officers and high school graduates who
made up the security forces of most companies. These men
were young to middle-aged, with a distinctly military bearing,
and Chant suspected they were members of R. Edgar Blake's
private army, probably trained in secret in Europe.

Chant's aerial reconnaissance had confirmed his belief that
by far the greatest concentration of security measures were
around the research-and-development facility, which was
fenced off from the other areas inside the complex, as well as
from the outside.

Those windowless buildings, Chant thought, were where
he would have to go.

It was seven-thirty in the evening by the time Chant finished
in the photo lab, and he left with a large manila envelope
filled with blown-up photographs under his arm. Using a pay
phone on the street, he called Jan at the motel where they were
staying to see whether she would prefer to have him bring
back food or go out to dinner, and was cheerfully informed
that she had already made arrangements for their dinner.

When Chant entered the motel suite, he was both surprised
and delighted to find a superb sushi buffet spread over the
surface of two writing desks, which had been pushed together.
The fresh fish and vegetables looked well chosen, and the
various dishes had been laid out to appeal to the eye as well as
to the palate. In a corner of the room, a pot of aromatic tea sat

on a hot plate Jan had apparently borrowed from the front office. Jan, beaming, stood in the center of the room; she was dressed in a sheer, beige negligee, which nicely complemented her blond hair and brown eyes, and flattered her shapely body.

"Very nice, Jan," Chant said with a smile and an appreciative nod. "Everything."

"Thank you, sir," Jan replied with a small curtsy. "I thought you would like sushi. I don't know why, but I always feel like there's something so *Japanese* about you."

"Really?"

"Yes, really. Anyway, I once took a course in sushi preparation and presentation. I hope it's all right."

"It looks superb," Chant said, pulling over chairs for them to sit in. He seated Jan, poured tea for both of them, then sat and sampled a few of the dishes with the chopsticks Jan had laid out. "It *is* superb."

"Thank you. They have delicious seafood all over here, and it was easy to get a bus just across the street. I hope you don't mind that I bought the negligee; I don't suppose it was really necessary."

Chant looked at her, laughed. "I love it. Buy whatever you want or need, just as long as you use the credit cards I gave you."

"I did—and I destroyed all of my own cards, just to be on the safe side in case my purse is stolen."

"Good. For now, you're Mary Gurran."

"How did you make out, Chant?"

Chant nodded toward the manila envelope on the bed behind them. "Those are the photographs I took. Later this evening or tomorrow, we'll see what they look like under a magnifying glass. It's a big complex, with a tough security force; you can bet there's a hell of a lot more going on in there than drug manufacturing and distribution. I need to find the best way to infiltrate the security, then get into both the administration offices in the center of the complex, and those windowless buildings to the northwest."

"Sounds exciting," Jan said lightly as she deftly slipped some fish into her mouth. "Incidentally, I got a job today."

"Oh?" Chant paused with his teacup halfway to his mouth. "I thought you were working for me."

"I am," Jan replied, pushing a plate of delicately sliced fish toward Chant. "That's why I got this particular job. Mary Gurran is going to be working as a file clerk in the offices of R.E.B. Pharmaceuticals. I start tomorrow."

"No," Chant said in a flat tone, setting his cup down. He turned in his chair, fixed Jan with his gaze. "Mary Gurran doesn't show up for work tomorrow—or any other day."

"Yes, she does," Jan replied, the firmness in her tone matching his. "It makes sense, and you know it."

Chant deliberately set aside his chopsticks and napkin, rose to his feet, and stared hard down at the woman. "Working for me is a risky business at best, Jan. You know that. For that reason, I make decisions as to what makes sense and what doesn't. People who work for me follow my instructions. You're fired. Keep those credit cards and the rented car until you get to wherever it is you want to go; I suggest you take a long, cross-country bus tour. Keep the name Mary Gurran for at least another month, by which time this matter should be finished and you'll be free to be whoever you want to be. When you no longer need the cards, please destroy them thoroughly."

Jan turned in her chair, crossed her legs, and spoke in a firm voice to Chant's back as he began packing his clothes in his suitcase. "You can fire me, Chant, but I'm still going to work in the offices of R.E.B. Pharmaceuticals; you can't stop me. And I'm not going anywhere. I have a job here in Houston, and—thanks to you—I have a perfectly good new identity. I'll get my own credit cards. You see, it doesn't make any difference what you do, or whether you fire me; I'm *still* going there. And if you care to stop back here at the motel from time to time in the next week or two, I will be more than happy to report to you what, if anything, I find out. If I discover anything particularly juicy in the files that it's my job to keep in order, I'll try to make copies for you. You may as well stop by to check out what I find, because—whether you come around or not—I'm still going to be digging through those files looking for the things you want to know. I'd hate to think all of my efforts will be in vain."

Chant slowly turned around to face her. "Why?" he asked quietly.

Jan shrugged. "Why what?"

"Jan, you know I don't want you to do this. Why do you persist?"

"You don't want me to do it because you think it's dangerous."

"I don't *think* it's dangerous, Jan; it *is* dangerous. You seem to forget that the last time we met it was in the company of a man with a machete who had it in mind to di.. you up like the fish we've been eating. And you weren't anywhere near as dangerous to R. Edgar Blake than as you are now; the people who'll be your co-workers work for him."

"I haven't forgotten. How could I forget something like that?"

"Jan, your disguise and your identity documents are adequate—unless someone really wants to run a check on you. If you make a mistake—just one, mind you—somebody may put a bullet in your brain; or worse. I repeat what I said last night; this business is not a game for a woman looking for something exciting to do because her last job bored her. This job as a filing clerk could literally bore you to death."

Jan felt herself flush with anger, but she remained sitting, breathing deeply, until the anger passed. John Sinclair, she thought, was a master of control, and if she were not to lose the man she loved in this greatest of gambles she had to demonstrate to him that she, too, knew how to remain calm. When she was sure she was once again in control of her emotions, able to think and speak clearly, she rose and slowly walked across the room until she was standing directly in front of him.

"That was a very insulting and hurtful remark, Chant," Jan

said evenly as she stared directly up into his eyes. "But I forgive you, because I understand why you said it. I wasn't bored with my job in New York—and you know that. I was desperately frustrated by my inability to effect any change in the lives of people I badly wanted to help. I came to believe that nothing I did made any real difference, and I was right; no matter what I did or how hard I worked, my clients kept on starving, getting bitten by rats, freezing in the winter, and roasting in the summer."

Jan paused, raised her right hand and gently placed it on Chant's massive chest. "I want to *work* for you, Chant—I want to make a difference, like you do. Please believe me when I say that the prospect of dying while I'm really doing something doesn't frighten me nearly as much as memories of the empty life I was leading. I once tried to kill myself, remember? You know I don't think of this as a game. I'll be careful, and I won't make mistakes. It's just an *office* job, for heaven's sake. Let me do it."

"I never use people on field operations," Chant said flatly, remembering an exception he had made with Alistair and how the old man had almost been killed. Remembering Martha.

"Look, a situation like this will never come up again. After this, I will be most happy to serve in John Sinclair's rear guard while he goes on with his solo operations around the world. But what I want to do at this time and in this place just makes sense. You need all the help you can get. When I went into their employment office, I could see that the entire complex is crawling with nasty-looking, armed guards. The place is guarded like a fortress."

"I'm well aware of that, Jan," Chant said dryly.

"I know you are, and *I'm* aware of the fact that you can—and even eventually will—get past all those men, the alarm systems, dogs, and whatever else they may have in there. But you're the one who told me that information is the most potent weapon. You also precisely instructed me that the objective in Houston was to infiltrate, gather information, then quietly retreat. So, through me, you've already infiltrated. I don't have a death wish, Chant; I'm not going to take any unnecessary risks. If I can't find anything in the files I'm assigned to work on, then that's that. But at least you'll still have a pair of eyes in there. I accept any risk there may be; there's no responsibility on your shoulders."

"You sound like Martha," Chant said, intending to shock. "Did I tell you that she and her husband were decapitated?"

"I heard it on the radio," Jan replied evenly. "This is a totally different situation, and I consider it a privilege to help, in whatever small way I can, find the people responsible for Martha's murder."

Chant shook his head. "Mary Gurran doesn't show up for work tomorrow—not if Jan Rawlings wants to keep working for me."

Jan smiled. "You already fired me, remember? Now, speaking of infiltration, while I was taking my interview, I learned that R.E.B. Pharmaceuticals is seriously short of laborers in their warehouse and loading operation. I happened to casually mention that I have a big, strong friend who'd just been laid off his construction job and is looking for work. They'd really like you to stop in and fill out an application, Mr. *Marsh*. If you do, you'll probably be working in the warehouse by tomorrow afternoon—that is, unless you'd prefer to be climbing over electrified fences and barbed wire, and padding tippety-toe past all those guards, instead of walking through the main gate."

Chant sighed, reached out and took Jan's hand in his. "You're getting to be a real pain in the ass," he said quietly.

"And besides being gutsy, persistent, and clever, I'm also pretty good in bed—at least with you. Right?"

"Indeed. Shall we finish our sushi and then pursue that subject?"

"No. Let's first pursue that subject, then finish the sushi."

CHAPTER FIFTEEN _____

THE TATTOOED CHUCK Politan was there, along with the other "graduates" from Chant's section of the project at Blake College; Chant was certain that the Greenblatts' murderer and Jan's attacker had come from this plant in Houston, and he wondered how many other men among the hundred or so working the three shifts were ex-convicts mixed in with people, like himself, hired off the street.

Using the name Tom Marsh, wearing horn-rimmed glasses with a bushy wig and false mustache, Chant had completed his disguise by walking with a slight limp and speaking with a trace of a Scottish brogue. Although he worked at close quarters with Politan and the other ex-convicts, no one had given the slightest hint of recognition. Satisfied after three days that he was totally accepted as just another laborer in the warehouse and the loading docks, Chant worked, waited, and watched.

And worried about Jan.

• • •

"I checked the names you gave me," Jan said. "You were right, of course—but I'd never have known the names and records were phony unless you'd told me. Each of those men has been given a completely new identity, including a phony Social Security number and an employment history dating back twenty years or so."

Chant nodded. "The men believe their pasts have been completely obliterated. Thinking that they have the opportunity for a fresh start, with good jobs and no criminal records, must be highly motivational—obviously, they pretty much manage to stay out of trouble. When Blake wants someone killed, for whatever reasons, one of those men is selected as the assassin. That man is abducted, put into a drug-induced hypnotic trance, and programmed somehow to kill the target subject. The man is sent off—or, more likely, taken—to a point of attack, then let off the leash. At that time, of course, his regular identity is restored to him. All of his records at R.E.B. are destroyed, so there's no way to trace him back here. They must do the drugging and programming in the closed-off section."

"My God, Chant, it's frightening . . ."

"Yes. Maybe it's time you resigned your position."

"No," Jan said defiantly. "When I said it was frightening, I didn't mean *I* was frightened. In fact, I made you a copy of those men's applications and phony records. Good stuff?"

"Good stuff," Chant said as he took the papers from Jan and placed them in a black leather briefcase. "How much risk was there for you in getting these? Be honest."

"No problem," Jan replied with a shrug. "These came right out of files I was assigned to work on."

"What about the copying?"

"I've been there a few days now, so I'm accepted. People are using the copying machines all the time, for one reason or another. I just slipped these in with some other files I had to copy."

Chant gently kissed the woman. "You be careful."

"I will, my dear. Don't worry."

• • •

Chant drove the huge forklift truck he operated over to a docking bay, shut it off, got down, and walked over to where the other men were taking their coffee break. He bought a container of black coffee from the vendor, sat down on a carton next to Chuck Politan.

"You drive that forklift pretty good, Marsh," Politan said with an approving nod.

Chant shrugged. "Been doing it most of my life."

"Yeah, well, fast isn't always good. I heard a story about a guy getting himself crushed under one of those things."

"Here?"

"Here. It happened sometime last summer. They say the guy had only been on the job a couple of weeks."

It could very well have been Ron Press, Chant thought; somehow, Blake or Hammerhead had found out about the letter the man had written. "I'll be careful to watch what I'm doing," Chant said evenly.

"Chant, they make everything here from aspirin to plant food, ship products all over the world, and their billings are enormous. It's incredible how many sole patents R.E.B. Pharmaceuticals holds. The profits are enormous—and they're legitimate, as far as I can tell. Why on earth should this R. Edgar Blake do things that are illegal? He doesn't *have* to!"

"Blake did a great many illegal things to get to his present position of wealth and power; corruption and killing can get to be habits. Also, I told you that, with Blake, evil is a kind of hobby. What about the gluteathin?"

"It's manufactured over in the research section, shipped directly from those loading docks. There isn't really that much of it made; it's incredibly potent in small doses, and highly controlled—for all intents and purposes, it totally cuts off a person from his own will and sensations."

"Do they manufacture any other controlled drugs over there besides GTN?"

"I don't know; I haven't been able to find out yet what else goes on in those labs. I do know that they use lots of animals, and that the people who work there don't mix with the rest of us. Those people come and go through their own separate gate."

Chant nodded. "I've seen."

"I know they have a separate payroll, and I can't find any records of it."

"They probably have a separate administration section there, and they keep their own records. Be careful what you look for."

"That's right."

"What do you mean, 'that's right'?"

"They do keep separate records for everything—I just haven't been able to gain access to them. And I'll tell you something else I know: the amount of GTN they make may be minuscule compared to all their other products, but they still make three times as much as they're licensed to."

Chant was silent for some time before he spoke. "How the hell did you find that out, Jan?"

The woman's brown eyes glowed as she smiled. "I have my ways." When Chant remained silent, she continued, "There's a computer terminal in the manager's office, and I know it's hooked up to another one in the research labs; it's how my boss Granger calls up information from that section without having to get up and go over there. Yesterday, I noticed that the cleaning people had dumped a whole load of computer printouts from Granger's office wastebasket into the communal trash bin—usually, Granger shreds them, but these were intact. At the end of the day, I managed to save a few things. There were too many to take out, and I didn't dare try to make copies, but I did manage to do some quick reading."

"You're going far too fast, Jan," Chant said, his voice low and intense. "And trying to do far too much."

"I realize that," Jan said evenly, "and I'm not going to do anything like that again. In fact, I have some news for you that you'll definitely like—but I have to tell you something else first, something I picked up from those sheets. By now, I recognize the chemical formula for GTN; the one-third of the stuff they manufacture under license is 'straight,' pure GTN. The illegal two-thirds, I'm sure, has something added to it. I have no idea what it is, because I'm not a chemist, but on the printouts you can see just a slight difference in the formulas —and the different chemical symbols are included in the GTN formula, but placed in parentheses."

Chant thought about it, nodded. "Physical amplification."

"Come again?"

"Physical amplification. They probably add steroids, amphetamines, that sort of thing. For a short period of time, whoever ingested the drug would not only be in a trance, but would have considerably greater physical strength; it would take more than one man, and probably more than one bullet, to put him down. It would explain how the assassins in both Rome and Switzerland managed to get to and kill their targets, despite the presence of bodyguards. Physical amplification would make these assassins human battering rams as well as mindless killers."

"But wouldn't things like GTN, steroids, and amphetamines show up in the bloodstream at an autopsy?"

"For GTN, a pathologist would probably have to know what he was looking for. Amphetamines, and any number of other drugs, would be expected, and nobody would pay attention. Finally, nobody has thought to do an autopsy. Why should they? These men are just crazed, ex-convict killers, right?"

"Right," Jan said, and shuddered. "That's all I was able to find out."

"You've done enough, Jan. You've already taken far too many risks. You've given me time on the inside to see the layout, and I think I know the best way to get into the research labs—from the inside, during the changing of a shift. You've done an absolutely marvelous job—but now it's time to get out. With no arguments."

Jan wrapped her arms around Chant's neck, went up on her toes and kissed his lips. "Surprise; I agree with you. I know when to quit—which is what I've done."

Chant smiled. "This is the news you told me I'd be happy to hear."

"That's it."

"You were right; I'm happy to hear it."

"I've given a week's notice—they wanted two, but I said I had a great job offer in Seattle and simply had to leave in a week."

"Why don't you just not show up, Jan?"

"I thought it would be wiser and safer in the long run if I did it this way; if I simply drop out of sight, somebody might get suspicious. By giving notice, they'll expect me to leave and won't think anything of it when I just walk out at the end of the week."

"You're certain that nobody's suspicious now?"

"I'm certain. As far as Granger is concerned, I've been nothing more than a model employee—and that is *all* I will be for five more days. Then I'll be safely out. All right?"

"All right."

With his forklift Chant raised a pallet of cartons bound for overseas off a loading platform, turned around, and gently eased them into the back of a truck. Then he turned off the engine and waited while his crew loaded another pallet. He watched idly while Hammerhead, an expensive gabardine overcoat draped around his shoulders, walked across the warehouse floor and stopped to confer with Uwe von Deck, the huge, solidly built chief of security at R.E.B. Pharmaceuticals. Once, Hammerhead turned around and glanced in Chant's direction, but gave no sign of recognition.

"Who's the ugly guy in the overcoat?" Chant asked one of the men inside the truck unloading the pallet.

The man looked up, glanced in the direction where Chant had nodded, grimaced slightly. "Oh, that's Mr. Wing."

"Who's he? I haven't seen him around here before."

The worker straightened up, arched his back, took off his cap and scratched his bald head. "I don't know what he does exactly, but I'm pretty sure he works for the big boys in Switzerland—the people who own this place."

"R.E.B. Pharmaceuticals is Swiss-owned?"

"That's what they say. In fact, you see all the tough-looking security guards around here? We call them the Swiss Army; they're trained in Switzerland. That von Deck is a fair guy, but he can be a mean son-of-a-bitch when he wants to be; he's the toughest of them all."

Not quite, Chant thought. The man talking to Uwe von Deck might not be the smartest or most stable man, but he was the toughest of all R. Edgar Blake's employees—and the most dangerous. It appeared that Blake had sent Hammerhead on another errand. "Why all the muscle?" Chant asked. "I don't see anything we ever load that would call for all the security."

"It discourages pilfering," the worker said, and laughed loudly. "Hey, I'm only half kidding; nobody steals anything out of this place, I'll tell you. And you don't see fights or shit like that. For some reason, we get some strange types working here. I remember one time one of these strange types started mouthing off to von Deck about something, and von Deck just about took his head off; knocked him cold with one punch. Him and his guys are good. Anyway, I think the real reason for the heavy security is because of the stuff they do over in the research section."

"What do they do in the research section?" Chant asked mildly.

The worker shrugged. "I haven't got the slightest idea; government work, I guess. It's secret."

Chant grunted, glanced once more in the direction of Hammerhead and Uwe von Deck, then started up the forklift.

"Chant, there's something funny going on there that I don't undersand; whatever it is has Granger and the other biggies all excited."

"Any chance they're on to the fact that you've been poking around?" Chant asked tersely.

Jan shook her head. "No. I think whatever it is involves a

man. Uwe was in and out of Granger's office all morning, and the door was always closed when they talked, but I did manage to pick up a few words here and there. I heard Uwe say something about 'keeping him locked up.' Then Granger said that wasn't good enough, that they had to know how he found out about the place."

Chant sat away from the others in the cavernous warehouse, sipping black coffee and once again going over in his mind his planned entry route to the research section. He had already purchased a uniform similar to those worn by the guards, brought it to the plant, and hidden it behind a stack of dusty pallets that looked as if they hadn't been moved in months. He would make his move the next day; he would stay behind after his shift ended and hide until dark, dress in the uniform, and cross the grounds to the power plant, where he would short out the circuits that fed power to the entire facility. In the ensuing confusion and darkness, he would enter the research section through a maintenance access tunnel that ran underground from the administration building to the laboratories.

In the meantime, Chant noted that Dale Reeves, one of the "graduates" from his section of the Blake College project, had not been to work for several days.

"Here, he was known as Arthur Hudley. He quit last week."

Chant shook his head. "None of those men are in a position to quit."

"I shouldn't think so."

Chant opened his briefcase, brought out the applications and employment records Jan had copied for him. He found a telephone number for Arthur Hudley, picked up the phone, and dialed it. A recorded voice informed him that the phone had been disconnected.

"I'm going over there," Chant said as he hung up the telephone. "But later tonight—after we celebrate your last day of work with dinner and a beverage of your choice."

"Good," Jan said, grinning. "But first, I have a present for you."

"Oh?"

Jan went into an adjoining room, reappeared a few moments later with a large package wrapped with red paper and a pink bow. Chant unwrapped the first box, only to find another inside. "Cute," he said as he bemusedly unwrapped the second package, and found a third inside that.

"I was alone in the office—you just keep on unwrapping! —for a couple of hours today when the idea for bringing you that little present occurred to me. There'd been an awful lot of activity—and loose talk—going on because of whoever it was that they caught. Granger's private phone line linking him to the research section was constantly ringing, and Uwe was running all over the place. Finally Granger just got disgusted and left—I assume he went over to Research. He left his office door unlocked. Now, I know I said I was going to be good, but this just seemed like too good an opportunity to pass up."

Chant opened the last, small package, found inside a single floppy computer disc. He glanced up at Jan with surprise and alarm.

"That's a copy of whatever Granger had loaded into that computer," Jan continued, "which means the payroll must be there, employees, shipping records—all of it. Don't worry; I left everything exactly as I found it. I'm computer literate, so I knew what I was doing, and the extra disc came from an opened carton in a supplyroom used by all the office employees. Nobody will notice a thing. I don't have the slightest idea of everything that's on there, but I figured you'd be interested in finding out. Are you pleased?"

Chant took Jan in his arms, brushed his lips against her hair. "I'm pleased. But now you're retired."

"Now I'm retired. Isn't that why we're going out to dinner?"

• • •

Chant called in sick the next day, went into downtown Houston and rented space in a temporary office center with a computer and printer.

Five minutes after he had broken the security code lock on the disc, Chant knew that Jan Rawlings had done all his work for him; he did not need to go into the research section, for everything he needed to know was on the disc—including a series of dates, one of which corresponded to the day on which Vito Biaggi had been shot, linked to names and sums paid in various currencies.

R. Edgar Blake had been renting out his assassination service, Chant thought; the names next to the days and sums of money would be those of people around the world who had availed themselves of it, for one reason or another. The name next to the date on which Vito Biaggi had been killed would be a master link in the chain his friend had been trying to break.

Safely away from Houston, there would be plenty of time to sort through all the voluminous information on the disc, glean what data would be useful to him for his next objective, and then send on the rest to various authorities, newspapers, and television networks around the world. Vito, he thought with a grim smile, would be pleased.

Now it was time to go back to England, where Jan would be safe and he could leisurely plan his assault on the fabled castle of R. Edgar Blake.

Chant made several copies of the disc, printed out typewritten copies of a terse report summarizing what the coded material undoubtedly contained. Two of the discs and reports he placed in manila envelopes, which he addressed to the Dallas office of the FBI and the Washington office of Interpol. He mailed the envelopes at the post office, then headed back to the motel. On the way the news came over the radio that a militant Southern union official had been knifed to death by an ex-convict named Dale Reeves, who had apparently run amok.

•   •   •

The door was open when Chant pulled into the parking space outside their motel suite. He hurried inside, and immediately knew that whoever had taken Jan were professionals, and good. He had probably only missed them by minutes, he thought, for the eye-watering smell of chloroform still hung in the air.

The room had been thoroughly ransacked and searched, but everything Jan had brought him had been in the briefcase he had taken to the office center; that much, he thought, was in their favor.

Chant took a series of deep breaths to relax his muscles and fight back the black tidal wave of anxiety that was welling in him. Then he took his loaded .45 from his briefcase, closed the door behind him. He lay down on the bed, put the .45 on his belly and his hands behind his head. If they had meant to kill Jan, Chant thought, then she was already dead, and if they had known about him, they would have set up an ambush. There was nothing to do now but wait until morning—or, if Jan were forced to talk, they made the mistake of coming back for him.

CHAPTER SIXTEEN _____

HIS SENSES FINELY tuned to the slightest nuance of tension in the people around him, Chant passed through the warehouse employees' entrance of R.E.B. Pharmaceuticals the next morning. There were two checkpoints where he had to show credentials, but at neither one did anybody give any indication that they had been waiting for him and that he was walking into a trap; none of the guards, including Uwe von Deck, looked at him suspiciously. It appeared, Chant thought, that he would have the freedom of movement he needed—at least for a little while longer.

Chant had decided that it was the last bit of business with the computer that had done Jan in; if the people at R.E.B. had been suspicious of the woman beforehand, she would have been detained at the plant. Her activity had been discovered later, after her last day, probably because she had triggered some kind of warning mechanism inside the computer that indicated that an unauthorized copy of a program had been made. The fact that Jan had been alone in the offices for part of the day had condemned her.

Chant knew that Jan would not betray him willingly, but it was only a matter of time before Blake's people, using a sophisticated combination of drugs, mental and physical torture, compelled her to reveal the identity of the man to whom she had given the computer disc and other information. And R.E.B.'s logs would show that he was in the complex . . .

He did not have a lot of time, Chant thought, and so he would waste none. The pile of pallets in which he had hidden his uniform had been moved during the night, but it made no difference; he had not planned to wait until the end of the shift. With Jan captured, finesse was a luxury he could no longer afford.

"I'd like to meet you in Warehouse D, Politan," Chant said to Chuck Politan in his normal voice, purposely not using the name Politan was going under in Houston.

The tattooed man stopped and quickly turned, frowned uncertainly. "What's up, Tom? Why did you call me—?"

"My name's not Tom, and I need to talk to you and the others around here who took part in the research project at Blake College. Try to get them to Warehouse D as soon as possible—now. You know who they are. Your lives depend on it. Trust me now, as you did once before when I told you you wouldn't die."

Politan's jaw dropped, and he stared at Chant. "Hey, your voice . . . you sound like that—"

But Chant was already walking away, very conscious of the fact that an alarm could be sounded at any moment, in which case dozens of guards would be converging on him.

He found the chief of security in his office, inside a small annex abutting the main administration building. "Excuse me, sir," Chant said in his Scottish brogue. "There's trouble in D."

Uwe von Deck quickly rose from his chair, reached down to his side, and unsnapped the flap on a holster holding a Colt revolver. "What's the matter, Marsh?"

"I think you'd better come and see for yourself."

With Chant limping along behind him, the burly security chief hurried across the grounds of the complex to Warehouse D, a storage facility with only one sliding metal door at the front and a standard door at the rear. The building was really nothing more than a large maintenance shed, and housed two gasoline pumps.

As they entered the shed through the front, Chant was relieved to see Politan and the others who had been with him at Blake College standing at the rear, in front of a pile of gasoline drums. The men were shuffling their feet as they nervously glanced at one another.

"All right," von Deck said sharply as he abruptly stopped walking. "Now, what seems to be the prob— Hey, what the hell?!"

Chant had pushed the lower button on a control panel near the entrance, and now the great metal door came crashing down, leaving the interior of the shed only dimly lit by four bare bulbs suspended from the ceiling.

"Each one of you is marked for death," Chant said in his normal voice, which echoed slightly inside the shed, carrying easily to the opposite end.

The guard started to grab for his gun. Chant's right fist shot straight out and hit von Deck in the right shoulder, directly over a major nerve cluster; the man's right hand spread open, and the Colt clattered to the concrete floor. The chief of security looked down at his paralyzed arm, as if he could not believe what had happened, then abruptly reached with his left hand across his body for his walkie-talkie. Again, Chant's fist shot out, and von Deck's left arm went limp. His face flushed with rage, the guard reared back and lifted his leg to deliver a powerful side kick. Chant, with speed that made his movements seem no more than a blur to the guard and ex-convicts watching, stepped inside the kick, spun, and brought his right elbow hard directly into the man's solar plexus; von Deck dropped like a stone to the floor, where he writhed, clutched at his stomach, and gasped for breath.

Chant unhurriedly bent down, took the walkie-talkie from

von Deck's belt, and picked up the gun. As the astonished ex-convicts slowly started to walk toward him, Chant stuck the Colt in his waistband, set the walkie-talkie on top of a nearby gasoline drum, then abruptly tore off his wig and mustache and tossed them aside.

"Holy shit," a man by the name of Roger Gray said. "Neil Alter."

"Not Neil Alter," Chant said, glancing at each of the men in turn. "That's not my name, any more than Tom Marsh is. My real name is John Sinclair. Some of you may have heard of me."

Politan, Gray, and one other man nodded; the two others simply gaped. Respect—and not a little fear—moved in the eyes of the men as they stared at the tall man with the iron-colored eyes and hair, a man they had all assumed was dead.

"The reason I became involved in this business in the first place is the same reason I'm here now," Chant continued evenly. "The man who owns both this plant and Blake College is responsible for the deaths of many innocent people, including a friend of mine. These people have been killed by men like you—ex-convicts carefully culled from a larger group of ex-convicts, then lured to places like this by promises of new identities, fresh starts, good jobs. Those promises were delivered on, but you weren't told the price you'd all have to pay. You're here for the sole purpose of forming a pool of unwitting assassins—men who, when the time comes, will be kidnapped, drugged, and hypnotized, then sent out like a zombie on a killing mission from which you won't return."

Chant paused, reached down and grabbed the front of Uwe von Deck's shirt, hauled the man to his feet. "Tell them I'm right, von Deck."

Still breathing hard, von Deck glared back at Chant, both fear and defiance in his dark eyes. Feeling had begun to return to his arms, and he feebly swung at Chant, who reached out and effortlessly caught the man's fist in his hand. "Just answer my questions, von Deck, and I won't hurt you again," Chant continued. "Resist me, and you're not going to have a chance to get your breath back. Am I telling these men the truth?"

The guard hesitated, glanced where Chant still held his fist in an iron grip, nodded. There were angry grunts from the other men, who had moved closer in a semicircle around Chant and von Deck. Chant quickly but calmly related the sequence of events that had brought him to Blake College. He told them about the deaths of the Greenblatts and Ron Press, the recent disappearance of Dale Reeves from their midst, and how Reeves had surfaced long enough to murder a union official before jumping to his own death from a highway overpass—and he told them about the capture of Jan. Through it all, the ex-convicts listened intently. Fear of Chant had vanished from their faces, but respect remained, and was intensified.

"Thanks, Sinclair," Roger Gray said, as Politan and the others nodded their affirmation.

"I would strongly suggest that you men split," Chant said. "You still come out ahead. The new identities and backgrounds these people have cooked up for you are fairly solid, and they can't very well blow the whistle on you without having to explain why they broke a number of federal and state laws to cook them up for you in the first place. You still have the chance to start new lives, as long as you don't get into trouble and have people doing deep background checks on you.

"If you're leaving now, you might consider doing a bit of trashing on the way out. I'm not talking riot, because there are too many guards. However, a fire here and there in the next twenty minutes might begin to pay them back for what they tried to do to you. Also, it would help me by providing a diversion; I'm going into the research section now to get the woman out before they damage or kill her."

If they hadn't already.

Chant's words were abruptly punctuated by crackling from the walkie-talkie sitting on top of the gasoline drum. The crackling stopped, and a voice—tense, urgent—came on. *"Intruder! Intruder! Red alert! Pick up Thomas Marsh in the*

*warehouse section! Bushy red hair and mustache, walks with
a limp! The man's a spy! Get him!"*

The ex-convicts glanced at one another, and Politan motioned for the others to come with him. They followed Politan to the rear of the shed, where they stood in a tight knot talking quietly but animatedly.

"Where are they keeping the woman?" Chant asked von Deck, placing his fingers on a nerve cluster at the base of the man's skull. "Tell me quickly."

"Preparation room," von Deck gasped, wincing as pain shot down through his chest at the same time as air seemed to leak out of his lungs.

"Tell me precisely how to get there after I go through this inside gate."

"Turn right—"

"No," Chant said, and pressed harder. The guard cried out, and Chant released the pressure slightly. "I'll know if you're lying; the next time you lie, I break both your collarbones. Think about that, because you know I'll do it."

"You're going to kill me anyway."

"No. Not if you tell me what I need to know."

"Commander von Deck, where are you?! We've got a spy on the grounds!"

"Remember, one more lie, and I start to break things. Now, simply and clearly, tell me how I get to this preparation room after going into the first building beyond the gate."

"It's in the first building," von Deck said in a defeated voice, lowering his head and wincing, as if in anticipation of more pain. "Immediately after entering the building, turn left and go to the end of that corridor. Then go right. The prep room is the first door on your right after you go through a set of swinging doors."

"Guard posts? Remember not to lie if you want the use of your arms for the next two or three months."

"It's hard to tell how many men may be on free patrol, walking around."

"Just answer the question. How many fixed stations?"

"Besides the one at the entrance gate, the only other fixed position in that part of the building is outside the preparation room."

"Which side of the swinging doors?"

"The other side."

"The preparation room is where you drug and hypnotize the subjects?"

The man nodded slightly, and Chant hit the security guard on the jaw with a straight right. The man crumpled to the floor, unconscious.

"Commander von Deck, where the hell are you!"

Without even glancing at the men who were still gathered in a knot, talking, Chant strode purposefully to the back of the shed, reached for the doorknob.

"Sinclair," Chuck Politan said, "wait a minute."

With his hand on the knob, Chuck turned toward the men, watched as Roger Gray and another man rolled two drums of gasoline toward the opposite end of the shed.

"You want a diversion, you'll get one hell of a diversion," Chuck Politan said with a broad grin that served to shrink the daggers on his cheeks. "You give the word, this shed goes up—and that's just for openers. We'll give the folks who run this place plenty to think about. When do you want her lit up?"

Chant nodded toward the unconscious security guard. "Take him out and put him in a safe place. He'll be out for at least a half hour, and I told him he wouldn't be killed if he told me what I wanted to know."

"But—"

"I want him out, Politan."

"He'll never know."

"I'll know. He won't be awake soon enough to be a threat to anybody. Besides, he's just an employee."

"Make sure you get von Deck out of here before you blow the place," Politan called to one of the other men, then turned back to Chant as Roger Gray walked over to join them.

"Chuck and I talked it over, Sinclair," Roger Gray said.

"You can use some help, and we're going in with you."

Chant shook his head. "I'll appreciate any diversion you can create, but I don't want anyone with me. You're both likely to get killed."

"What?" Politan said in mock dismay. "You think you can dodge bullets any better than we can?"

"Yes," Chant replied simply. "Stay in this section long enough to do what you want to do, then get out."

Politan and Gray glanced at one another, seemed to reach some kind of mutual, unspoken conclusion between themselves. It was the man with tattooed daggers on his cheek who voiced it.

"Sooner or later Roger and I would have been dead anyway, Sinclair, if not for you and the lady," Chuck Politan said. "You got the guts to go in there after her, then Roger and I have the guts to run interference for you. The other guys will provide plenty of excitement for the guards. You're wasting time by arguing with us."

Chant nodded slightly, then turned toward the other men, one of whom was holding a book of matches. At his feet was a puddle of gasoline with liquid tributaries leading to at least a dozen other drums of gasoline, which the two other ex-convicts were busy opening. Gasoline was splashing on the concrete floor, spreading . . .

"One minute," Chant said curtly, glancing at his watch. "You're going to have quite a blast here, so make sure you leave yourselves time to get out—and make sure that you take von Deck with you."

"We'll do what you say, Sinclair," the man standing over the spreading puddle of gasoline said. "You've got one minute from now . . . go. And good luck. Chuck, Roger—good luck."

Politan and Gray grabbed pickaxes from a pile of rusting tools, followed Chant through the door, and flanked him as he started to walk across the grounds toward the gate in the electrified fence surrounding the research section. Chant glanced at his watch, saw that he had fifty-five seconds. Security guards were running in all directions, searching. Two guards saw them emerge from the maintenance shed, stopped abruptly, and studied them.

"Just keep walking," Chant said in a low voice, angling away from the guards. "Make out as if nothing is wrong. They're looking for a lone man with bushy red hair and a mustache."

Using his peripheral vision, Chant watched as the two guards turned away and ran off in opposite directions. He glanced at his watch . . . thirty seconds. The gate to the research section was a little less than forty yards away.

Twenty seconds.

Chant picked up the pace slightly, angling toward the gate. The two men flanking him, pickaxes on their shoulders, unhesitatingly followed, imitating Chant's casual manner and stride.

Ten seconds.

Chant suddenly turned at a sharp angle, pulling the two other men with him, and started walking directly toward the gate, which was guarded by two men with Skorpion machine pistols. The guards looked up, exchanged startled glances at the sight of the three men striding purposefully toward them, then started to raise their machine pistols.

Suddenly the ground shook as Warehouse D exploded a hundred yards away.

Chant leaped forward, followed a split second later by Politan and Gray. A secondary explosion shook the ground again as Chant's right fist came up under the jaw of the guard on the left. Chant ducked low under a burst of machine-pistol fire, spun, and brought his heel crashing into the other man's sternum, crushing his chest and killing him instantly.

Politan raised his pickax in the air, brought it crashing down on the heavy lock on the gate. Sparks flew, but the electricity did not pass through the wooden handle. Sirens began to wail, the piercing sound coming from all directions, as Roger Gray struck at the lock with his pickax. More sparks flew, but the gate sprang open. Chant leaped through the opening a fraction of a second before a hail of bullets from an automatic weapon ripped through the space where he had been standing. Gray suddenly cried out in agony, spun around, and fell as bullets tore through his chest.

Chant, with Politan running beside him, sprinted the fifteen yards from the gate to the entrance of the first windowless building. Suddenly two guards appeared in the doorway directly ahead of them, Skorpions raised. Without breaking stride, Chant pulled the Colt from his waistband, aimed and squeezed off two rounds. Holes opened in the foreheads of both guards, and they fell backward, their weapons firing harmlessly into the air.

"Grab the other one!" Chant snapped as he scooped up one of the guards' automatic pistols. "We're going left! You watch our backs!"

Politan dropped his pickax and grabbed the second Skorpion, then raced after Chant. Chant, sprinting ahead, suddenly heard shots behind him. He dived, rolled, came up on his feet facing in the other direction with the Colt in one hand and the machine pistol in the other. Chuck Politan was kneeling in the center of the corridor, trading bursts of fire with a guard who had appeared from a doorway behind them. Suddenly the ex-convict cried out and clutched at his stomach as bloody holes exploded open in his back. As he fell forward, Chant fired a single round from the Colt into the guard's throat. As the guard spun around and fell back into the room, Chant stepped back against the wall, turned, and used the Skorpion to cut down a guard who had suddenly appeared at the end of the corridor.

Now Chant waited, a weapon pointed in each direction. He could hear the continuing scream of sirens outside the building. Then there was the dull thud of two more explosions, spaced a few seconds apart—automatic weapons fire and pistol shots. The ex-convicts had been true to their word, Chant thought; the two who had come with him had sacrificed their lives, and the three left outside were certainly creating a diversion—he could only hope they would survive amidst the deadly chaos they had wrought.

Suddenly, his keen hearing picked up the sounds of running, booted feet. Still, he waited; the sound moved off in another direction. When twenty seconds passed and no more guards appeared, Chant pushed off the wall and darted to the end of the corridor, where he stopped and peered around the corner, to his right. Twenty-five yards away, two guards burst through the swinging doors Uwe von Deck had mentioned, came running up the corridor. Chant waited, listening to the sound of their approaching footsteps, until they were almost to the corner, then stepped out in front of them and brought the Colt and Skorpion crashing into the sides of their heads. Unconscious while still on their feet, the two guards wobbled forward until they bumped into a wall, crumpled to the floor. Chant tossed the Colt away, ejected the empty clip from his Skorpion, reloaded with a fresh clip from the belt of one of the guards, picked up the second machine pistol.

Again he waited, crouching with Skorpions in both hands, as he looked down both corridors, listening. There were no sounds except the sirens and continuing explosions outside, and the corridors remained empty. Chant slowly straightened up and allowed himself a thin smile as it occurred to him that R.E.B. Pharmaceuticals had probably run out of guards, at least in this area of the research section; whoever was left would be out fighting fires, hunting saboteurs, guarding other entrances.

He turned to his right and, keeping close to the wall, moved silently down the corridor to the swinging doors. He opened one of the doors a crack with the barrel of one machine pistol, saw that the chairs behind the desk that served as a guard post were empty. He pushed through the doors, slipped into the first room on his right.

He found himself in a kind of small amphitheater, which looked like a screening room. There was a large screen covering the front wall, and twin film projectors sat on an elevated platform at the rear. Racks against the wall opposite him were filled with metal canisters, which Chant assumed contained film and videotape of various target subjects—past, present, and possibly future. Just inside the door, to his left, a large, white cabinet was stocked with hundreds of green capsules nestled in individual styrofoam pockets. Also against the near wall were racks of hypodermic needles, television monitors, and an array of medical paraphernalia. There were straight-backed chairs near all the walls, and four anchored leather recliners placed in a square in the center of the floor, facing the screen; each of the recliners was equipped with built-in leather restraining straps.

Jan, unconscious and with fluids from two different suspended bottles dripping through rubber tubes into veins in her arms, lay strapped into one of the recliners, which was laid out at full extension. Her flesh was deathly pale against the rich brown of the leather, and her white hospital gown was soaked with sweat. A white plastic cap covered her hair. Her mouth hung open, and when Chant pulled back her lids he found her eyeballs rolled back into her head. If it were not for Jan's rapid, labored breathing, Chant would have thought her dead.

The chair directly behind her was also occupied; strapped into it was the man Chant assumed had caused the executive-and-security furor of the past few days. The man's thinning hair was sweat-pasted to his forehead, and he was straining against the straps, gaping at Chant in wide-eyed disbelief.

"Jesus Christ, I was right," Duane Insolers gasped hoarsely. "John Sinclair."

CHAPTER SEVENTEEN _____

"THEY OVERDOSED HER," Insolers said, straining against his straps and craning his neck in order to watch Chant as he quickly undid the straps around Jan's chest, stomach, wrists and arms, ankles. "It happened just a while ago. They'd been working on her all night trying to get her to say who she was working with. She's a tough lady, that one; even drugged to the gills, she resisted. Finally, they just gave her too much shit."

"You're lucky you're otherwise occupied right now," Chant said evenly as he carefully removed the needles from Jan's veins. "If you weren't, I'd kill you."

"I'm not in any way responsible for her being here, Sinclair. And I'm not responsible for, or involved in, this aspect of the program; I just found out about it myself a couple of days ago. Look, for Christ's sake; I'm strapped down too!"

"But not doped up. You somehow got yourself in trouble with your boss, and now they're getting ready to do a number on you. Considering the job Tommy Wing did on Montsero and Tank Olsen, I'm perfectly willing to leave you to his tender mercies."

"I don't work for Blake."

"You're full of shit," Chant replied easily as he checked Jan's pulse, then massaged her arms and legs in an effort to improve circulation. She was very close to death, he thought, his mind already grappling with the problem of what story to tell when he took her to the nearest hospital emergency room.

"I'm telling you the truth, Sinclair. I really *do* work for the Central Intelligence Agency. It's true I was running a game on you when we first met, but that was standard procedure with all the subjects coming into the program—as I'm sure you figured out when you ran your own game on Tank Olsen. But I *am* a CIA operative. The reason they haven't really worked me over is because there's nothing I know that they don't already know. They want me undamaged for use as a possible bargaining chip."

"Bargaining chip for what?"

"The project was Company-sponsored—but never this aspect of it. Thanks to you, Sinclair, I finally found out what they've been doing here. The people at Langley are going to go apeshit if and when they find out what Blake's been up to. That's why I'm strapped in this chair; they're keeping me on ice until Blake decides what he wants to do with me."

"I still say you're full of shit."

"Let me loose, Sinclair," Insolers said as Chant lifted Jan in his arms and headed toward the door. "For Christ's sake, you can't get out of here by yourself; you can't even fire those guns accurately while you're holding the woman in your arms. I know the best way out—right through this section to the loading docks adjacent to the highway. I can show you the way. You'll never make it without me."

"I'll take my chances," Chant replied over his shoulder.

"Sinclair! *Cooked Goose!*"

Chant abruptly stopped at the door, slowly turned. His eyes searched Insolers's thin, rodentlike face. "What does it mean?" he asked softly, after a pause.

"I don't know," Insolers answered quickly. "Probably less than a half dozen men in the Company do know—but whatever Operation Cooked Goose was all about, it was the CIA operation that caused you to walk away from the war in Southeast Asia. You're the only person outside the top echelon of the Company who knows what Cooked Goose was all about —which is why they want you dead. *That* I know. They wanted you dead from the beginning, but even more so now. You've become a kind of legend; the more that legend grows, the more Langley worries you're going to be captured and wind up in a prison cell writing your memoirs. They'll never stop coming at you. I wouldn't know the little I do about you and Operation Cooked Goose if I weren't CIA, Sinclair. Right now you need me if the two of you are going to have any chance of getting out of here alive, so undo these straps."

"Where did you see or hear those words in the first place?"

"I saw them in a file on you; it just mentioned the operation's code name, not what it was about. Come on, Sinclair, you're wasting time. And you'll also be wasting time if you take her to a hospital; the woman could be dead by the time you finish explaining and filling out papers." Insolers paused, nodded in the direction of the white cabinet with its cargo of hundreds of green capsules. "She needs a Company doctor if she's to survive with her mind intact. I can get you to a Company safe house and have doctors there in the time it would take you to get her admitted to a hopsital—where, I don't have to tell you, you're going to attract a lot of attention. I'm offering you a truce, Sinclair. Accept it, and save the woman's life—and maybe your own."

Whatever else he was, Chant thought, Duane Insolers had to be CIA; it was the only way he could know as much as he did about Cooked Goose. That being the case, it was true that he probably offered the best chance to save Jan's life—if he could be trusted.

Chant went back into the room, eased Jan down onto one of the recliners, quickly freed Insolers.

"Give me one of the guns!" Insolers snapped as he leaped

from the chair. "I'll take the point; just follow me."

Chant tossed Insolers one of the machine pistols. Insolers grabbed the Skorpion out of the air, quickly and expertly checked the magazine, then bounded to the door, where he glanced up and down the corridor.

"Let's go, Sinclair," Insolers continued. "Right now, it looks like everybody's busy outside."

As Insolers stepped out into the corridor, Chant quickly reached into the cabinet, grabbed a handful of the green capsules, and slipped them into his pocket. Then he again lifted Jan in his arms and, gripping the machine pistol in his right hand, hurried after Insolers.

Insolers, who had paused ten yards down the corridor to the right to wait for Chant, now led the way through a second set of swinging doors, out an exit and through a small, open courtyard, then into another building on the opposite side. They moved through a labyrinth of narrow corridors, past empty offices and laboratories, into the heart of the research section. Insolers stopped before a set of steel doors, held up his hand. Chant came up beside him, stopped.

"The transportation pool and garage," Insolers said, his eyes constantly darting back and forth, looking for guards. "No matter what's happening in the rest of the complex, there are going to be some guards in there. But if we can make it out of the garage, there's only one gate to crash to get to the highway. When I kick the door open, you go through and run down the catwalk to your right; I'll try to give you plenty of cover fire. There are cars at the end of the garage, and they leave the keys in them. Get in the back of the blue Buick. I'll be right behind you, and I'll drive."

"Why that particular car, Insolers?" Chant asked curtly.

"It has a car telephone."

"Having you able to talk into a telephone doesn't sound like a good idea to me."

"Come on, Sinclair," Insolers said impatiently. "I don't care if the rumors about you being a universe-class *ninja* are true or not; right now, you've literally got your hands full, and if I wanted a quick promotion of about three grades I'd have blown off your head with this machine pistol the moment you stepped out of the prep room. I need a telephone to call ahead so the people in the safe house can make preparations. It will take about forty minutes to get there—about as long as it will take Company doctors to get there and set up whatever they need to flush the shit out of the woman's system. You want to waste forty minutes? I told you we have a truce; I'm not going to try to turn you in or trap you. You have no choice but to trust me. The agency has no idea that you're with me, and there won't be any other field operatives in the house; no one there will recognize you, and they probably don't know any more about John Sinclair but what they read in the news-papers. Once we get out of here, I'll drop you off at the first corner, before I make the call. If that's what you want."

"You know damn well I'm not going to leave the woman," Chant said evenly. "Hit the door."

Insolers kicked open the steel door to the left, immediately knelt down in firing position. Chant cut past the man's right shoulder through the door, found himself looking out over a cavernous garage. The multiple doors at the far end were all open, and through them Chant could see a wide driveway blocked by a double gate; beyond the double gate was a high-way. Three security guards at the opposite end of the garage had spun around at the sound of the door crashing open. They raised their Skorpions, simultaneously opened fire with In-solers.

Chant, his body twisted slightly to one side to shield Jan as much as possible, sprinted to his right along a narrow, con-crete catwalk six feet or so above the floor of the garage. At the far end six cars were parked next to each other, facing the garage entrance. The blue Buick was the last car. Ignoring the stairs at the end of the catwalk, Chant leaped nimbly from the catwalk onto the roof of the Buick, down onto the trunk, and finally to the floor. He jerked open the rear door, carefully laid Jan down on the backseat.

He backed out of the car and, using the car frame as a

shield, fired off a burst from his machine pistol that tore through the neck of one of the guards. Now Insolers, keeping low and firing as he ran, came sprinting down the catwalk as chunks of concrete flew from the wall behind and above him. When the two remaining guards started to run to their left to gain better firing position, Chant pulled the trigger on his Skorpion and cut them down. Insolers reached the car, jerked open the front door, and slid behind the wheel as Chant dived into the back.

Insolers turned the key in the ignition, and the powerful engine roared to life. He slammed the car into gear, and the Buick leaped forward, tires screaming along with the engine. The car shot out through one of the doors. Insolers kept accelerating as they headed up the driveway through the gates, and just before the Buick tore through both metal shields Chant lay down on top of Jan, shielding her body with his. The impact of the car with the second gate turned the car completely around, but Insolers straightened it out, and the car kept going despite the fact that vision through the cracked front windshield was now partially obscured by the twisted hood. At the end of the driveway Insolers twisted the wheel hard, and they careened onto the highway. To Chant's amazement, the car continued to run.

"Let's just hope the car keeps running," Insolers shouted back over his shoulder as he eased off on the accelerator and brought their speed down to a steady fifty-five, "and that the state police don't stop us; I hate to think of what this car looks like from the outside."

"Show them your CIA credentials."

"Blake's people took them away."

Insolers reached down for the phone in the padded console between the front seats, picked up the receiver, grunted with satisfaction when he found it working. He tensed slightly when he felt the bore of Chant's machine pistol touch the back of his neck, but he didn't hesitate in using the phone. He gave numbers that Chant recognized as a coded call sign. There was a short pause filled with static, which Chant could hear from the backseat, then three soft clicks. Insolers gave a code word, then his name. After another pause, more static, and three more soft clicks, he began speaking.

Chant listened carefully, but he could detect nothing in Insolers's voice or words that would indicate more code usage, and—most important—he did not hear his name mentioned. Insolers quickly explained that he had a sick woman with him who would need immediate treatment upon their arrival. He mentioned that she was suffering from GTN poisoning, then hung up the telephone.

"There'll be a medical team, with all the necessary equipment and supplies, at the house when we get there," Insolers said. He reached down, picked up the machine pistol on the seat beside him by its barrel, handed it back to Chant. "Here, this may make you feel better."

"Not necessary," Chant said easily as he took the machine pistol from Insolers and placed it on the floor of the car. "I only need one bullet in one gun to kill you if I don't like what happens next, Insolers. You may get John Sinclair in a trap he can't escape from, but you'll be receiving your three-grade promotion posthumously."

Insolers's response was to laugh. Chant smiled wryly, then leaned back in the seat and absently stroked Jan's hair. He found he liked the man who smelled like a medicine chest, respected him after seeing how he handled himself under fire. He also found, against all common sense, that he tended to trust Duane Insolers.

Which didn't mean that he'd let down his guard.

Thirty-seven minutes later Insolers drove through an open gate onto a winding dirt road crossing what appeared to be a small ranch. At the end of the road was a sprawling ranch house, and as they approached a large door in an attached garage swung open. Chant lifted up his machine pistol.

Insolers drove at full speed up the steeply inclined driveway, only braking at the last moment as the car entered what turned out to be a vast garage. The door slammed shut behind them, triggering banks of floodlights all around them. At least a half dozen men and women, one of them pushing a hospital gurney, came running toward the car.

Chant pressed the bore of the machine pistol against the back of Insolers's bucket seat as both of the Buick's back doors were yanked open. A heavyset man in a white lab coat reached in from the left and, ignoring the machine pistol, brusquely pushed Chant aside. He grabbed Jan under the armpits, pulled her from the car, and lifted her in his arms.

"I've got her on this side!" the man shouted in a firm, commanding voice that boomed in the vast, concrete-lined garage. "Bring that gurney around here!"

Two women in white lab coats rolled the gurney around from the other side of the car, helped the man ease Jan down onto it. Jan was strapped down, a needle from a suspended bottle of plasma inserted into a vein.

Chant found that he was being totally ignored.

"All right!" the big man with the booming voice shouted. "Let's get her upstairs!"

With one person guiding each side of the gurney, the medical team raced down the length of the garage to a wide door, which sighed open to reveal a large freight elevator. The team pushed the gurney into the elevator, and the door immediately closed behind them.

Everything had happened in less than forty-five seconds. Chant was impressed.

Insolers got out of the car and, without even looking back, headed toward the elevator. Chant checked the magazines of both machine pistols and took the one with the most ammunition left; but he put on the safety catch before getting out and following the CIA operative, who was holding open the elevator door for him.

CHAPTER EIGHTEEN ⸺

INSOLERS HUNG UP the wall telephone and turned to face Chant, who was standing directly behind him. "You certainly do like to stay close by, don't you, Mr. Jones?" the slight, tall man said with a thin smile.

Chant, certain even before Insolers had earlier put a finger to his lips that the entire safe house would be wired for sound, said nothing; for him, it was enough that the CIA operative was aware that his neck would be broken an instant after Chant suspected a trap was being set or sprung.

"That was one of the doctors calling from the medical suite," Insolers continued. "Miss Rawlings is going to be all right. They've flushed all of the drugs out of her system, and there doesn't appear to be any permanent brain or kidney damage. She should be well in two or three weeks, and we'll keep her here until she's completely healed. You can see her in an hour, after she wakes up, but she probably won't recognize you. It will take time for everything to come back to her."

Chant's reaction was to nod, reach out, and grip the other

man's arm as he allowed his gratitude to show on his face and in his eyes.

"You want a drink, Jones?" Insolers asked. He shrugged when Chant shook his head, continued, "Well, I do. If you're going to stay close, you'll have to come along with me."

Chant followed Insolers as the operative climbed a circular staircase to the second floor of the house, entered a well-appointed drawing room and library off the main corridor. Insolers closed the door, then went across the room and removed a thick volume from a bookcase. He reached inside the space, then removed his hand and replaced the book.

"It's all right to talk now, Sinclair. This room is used for 'clean' talk, and I just turned off the tape system here."

"What are you going to tell your superiors about the one-sided conversations on the rest of the tapes?" Chant asked as the other man went to a sideboard and poured himself a stiff drink from a bottle of bourbon.

"Beats me," Insolers replied as he dropped some ice inside his drink and raised his glass to Chant. "Maybe I'll tell them I've begun talking to myself."

"Why are you so solicitous of my well-being, Insolers?"

"For one thing, I owe you my life," Insolers replied easily. "At the very least, they'd have badly compromised me; if you'd gotten away, I believe they almost certainly would have killed me."

"You know I damn near left you there."

"But you didn't." Insolers paused, lifted his chin slightly and narrowed his eyes. "Anybody who really knows anything about you knows that you're a man of honor, Sinclair. I respect you—and so does virtually everyone else at the agency, even if they do happen to want you dead. I told you we had a truce; I'll let you know when the truce is over, and it won't be at a time when you're in jeopardy. Maybe I want you to respect me as a man of honor, too; maybe it's just possible that having John Sinclair's respect is worth more to me than a three-grade promotion."

"Awarded posthumously."

"Awarded posthumously," Insolers said, and laughed.

Chant nodded toward the sideboard. "I see you've got a bottle of single-malt Scotch over there. I'll have some of that, on the rocks."

Insolers made Chant a drink, brought it to him, then sat down in one of the four leather armchairs in the room. Insolers motioned for Chant to sit in a chair across from him, and Chant did.

"The Blake College thing was a CIA project from its inception," the operative said, lighting a cigarette and tossing the match into the fireplace behind him. "It goes back twenty years, testing different kinds of questionnaires and techniques. Blake and the insurance companies provided us with a front —not that unusual an arrangement, as you well know. Montsero was a renegade psychologist who got thrown out of UCLA for running unauthorized deception experiments— which he was doing for us, naturally.

"It's all part of Special Weapons research, and it was always designed to test the ongoing *feasibility* of using unwitting assassins who couldn't be traced back to the government. We were doing it because we had—have—good reason to suspect that other governments are doing it. The government of the United States never used one of those men, Sinclair, and didn't intend to—unless somebody else sent a similar type of assassin against us first. As far as we knew, all of the subjects who made it through to the final phase of the tests were paid their fees at that military base and then sent on their way."

"You never tested GTN on any of the men?"

"Nope; never had to. GTN is very effective, but we've got even better shit than that locked away and ready for use if we ever feel we need it. We know what those drugs can do, because they've been tested on Company volunteers. As far as the CIA was concerned, the Blake College operation was just a feasibility study and a means of keeping on hand a kind of stockpile of potential subjects. I'm still trying to put it all together, but the way I figure is that Montsero was the one who whispered something in someone's ear about the potential for using subjects to further Blake's personal political and economic interests. Blake liked the idea, and their own operation was set up right under our noses—my nose, really—without Company knowledge or authorization. Then you came along.

"I had two jobs. First, just as I did with you, I contacted every man and gave him that little spiel. The idea was to test loyalty patterns and dependability, but it was really just a side-show—more data for Company computers. My most important assignment was to vet every person entering the program to screen out any potential enemy agents. You weren't expecting any kind of thorough check when you penetrated the program, so you were blown fifteen minutes after I started checking out the application forms you'd filed; I found the real Neil Alter in Orlando, working for his brother selling condominums.

"So the question became who you really were, and who you were working for. Naturally, I figured you for an enemy operative, possibly Russian. You weren't going anywhere. I figured I could nab you whenever I wanted, so I 'dusted' you, wired your room, bugged your telephone, and did a few other things I thought would help me penetrate your operation and nab your controller. In the meantime, I let you roam free.

"Then, just before the last of the trials on the military base, I got snookered. I got word that I was to return to Washington for a meeting that never took place. The next thing I know, Montsero, an ex-convict, and a prominent couple have been butchered, and everybody and their goddam brother is going to New York City to hunt the infamous John Sinclair.

"I didn't believe you were John Sinclair—or, if you were, I didn't believe you'd done the killings. Sinclair might well have filleted Montsero and the other guy, but not an old man and an old woman. I smelled a whole stableful of rats. I still had you 'dusted,' and I had a miniature radio transmitter sewn into a pair of your pants, so I didn't feel the need to rush out and tell anybody where you were; there were too many people involved in the manhunt, somebody was bound to screw up, more people might be killed, and you'd be gone. I still wanted to know who you really were, and who'd sent you.

"I found you with the Rawlings woman, did some more checking and found out that you'd been referred to her by Martha Greenblatt. I also had an autopsy performed on the guy you killed in the welfare office; they found the GTN in his system, and I knew there was a good likelihood it had been manufactured here. For the first time I began to suspect that it had been Blake, or men working on his orders, who had offed Montsero and the others. I also began to consider the possibility that you really were John Sinclair—and that possibility intrigued me no end. After I searched your room in the house in Rockland County and found the passports and other stuff, I decided there was no longer any doubt who you were. But I was still in no hurry to turn you in, since now I wanted to know why *you* were involved—and you seemed to be doing all my work for me." Insolers paused, smiled wryly. "When I wanted you, I figured all I had to do was look one or two steps ahead of me.

"Then I lost you—or thought I did—when you slipped past my men in Rockland. Houston was on my schedule anyway, and I must have gotten there a week or so after you. I got into the research section at R.E.B. by using a forged letter that had Blake himself introducing me as a research chemist. I had great fun juggling test tubes while I faked that one, and it gave me time and freedom to do a lot of looking around." Insolers paused, shrugged. "I figured out what they were up to, and how they did it, but they nailed me before I could do anything about it. It's a good thing I never blew the whistle on you, or I might not be here. Now, speaking of promotions, somebody has to take credit for exposing Blake's operations and busting up that place in Houston. With your permission, Mr. Sinclair —and since I assume you don't wish your name to be bandied about—I'll take credit. Is that all right with you?"

"It's more than all right with me. You're a good man, Insolers."

"*You're* a good man; like I said, you did most of my work

for me. Maybe another reason I declared a truce is because
I've noticed, over the years, that John Sinclair and I happen to
intensely dislike a lot of the same people."

"Like R. Edgar Blake?"

"Like R. Edgar Blake. Why do they call you 'Chant,' Sinclair?"

Chant smiled, shrugged. "It's just a nickname."

"I've seen your dossier—at least I've seen the scrubbed
version most field operatives get to see. It says that some of
your men started calling you that back in 'Nam; it says that it
could have had something to do with the reactions of enemy
soldiers."

"It's not important, Insolers," Chant said quietly.

"What about Cooked Goose, Sinclair? What the *hell* was
that operation all about?"

"You don't want to know. If they ever suspected I'd told
you, you'd be a dead man. Wait until you get your three-grade
promotion; then you may be able to read all about it yourself."

"There may not even be a file on it."

"That's true. When the men who know about it now die,
the secret may die with them. It's just as well."

Insolers studied Chant for some time, finally said, "After
all these years, you've never told anybody what it was that
made you desert. And yet, they still want to kill you. Why?"

"They must be afraid I'll change my mind one day. And I
may. Tell me about Tommy Wing, Insolers."

The CIA operative looked surprised. "How the hell do you
know about that madman?"

Chant smiled without humor. "Oh, Hammerhead and I go
back a lot of years. He's the one who made me in the project;
and he may be the man who tripped you up in Houston. He
seems to be some kind of supervisor."

"Hammerhead?" Insolers said, and laughed. "Good name."

"You know about his tooth-fairy number?"

"I heard about it."

"Tommy bites people he doesn't like—usually to death.

Maybe he's cleaned up his act—washed his teeth of it, so to speak."

Insolers shook his head. "He hasn't. Sinclair, I know you once ran a scam on Blake. How well do you know him?"

"Only by his deeds and reputation."

"He's a very strange man, Sinclair. He looks like a big, old crow, and in his own way he's probably as criminally insane as Tommy Wing. I'm told he's gotten worse over the years. That castle he lives in dates back to medieval times, and there are rumors that some very strange things go on in there for his amusement. The castle and grounds cover a lot of expensive Swiss acreage, and nobody really knows what he does with it all. Some of it may be used to train—and discipline—the top members of his private army, but that's never been confirmed by the CIA. Anyway, some of the rumors are gruesome. It seems he's a collector of bizarre instruments of death and torture."

"Tommy Wing would fit nicely into that category," Chant said in a flat voice.

Insolers smiled. "Obviously. Wing was in the Blake College program, two and a half years ago. He took the field trials quite seriously and ended up killing two men in the pit. It looked like there was going to be a problem, so Montsero told Blake what had happened and asked for instructions. Blake got a big kick out of it, and had Tommy Wing flown to Switzerland for a personal interview. Now Wing serves as the old man's primary bodyguard, personal secretary, and general 'gofer.' As it turns out, Wing was also Blake's man in charge of security for the Blake College project—something I was never told about."

"Tommy's really come up in the world," Chant said dryly.

"Now you're going after Blake and Wing, aren't you?"

"That's something I really don't think you want confirmed or denied, Insolers. Whatever I'm going to do, it's better that you don't know about it."

"I can't help you on that."

"I don't recall asking you for help."

Insolers was silent for some time. Finally he rose, went to the sideboard, and poured himself a drink. He raised the bottle of single-malt Scotch inquiringly, but Chant shook his head.

"It occurred to me that you might figure the CIA would want to get even with Blake for going way out of bounds with our research project and using it for his own purposes."

"What the CIA wants to do about Blake doesn't interest me one way or the other," Chant replied evenly.

"Okay. Still, I thought you might be interested in learning a few more things about Blake which you probably don't know. R. Edgar Blake is much more than just your average run-of-the-mill multibillionaire. I told you he provided us with a front at Blake College, but that was only one of a number of front organizations around the world he provides for us, and for most of the other Western intelligence agencies. He's been of invaluable help to the CIA, like certain very wealthy individuals and multinational corporations before him. In exchange, of course, his companies get any number of lucrative government contracts."

"And protection?"

"He doesn't need our protection. The man knows an enormous amount about CIA covert operations, past and present, around the world. Virtually every intelligence agency in the West has had occasion to use Blake's facilities or help at one time or another, and in effect we've sold our souls to the devil. He's got very damaging stuff on all of us, which makes him virtually a world power unto himself. He has all the information he's collected inside one of the most sophisticated computer systems in the world, inside one of the world's most highly defended fortifications."

"What do the Swiss think of all this?"

Insolers laughed. "Are you kidding? With all that money? The Swiss love him! He's careful not to break any Swiss laws, and the taxes he pays probably account for half the budget of the city of Geneva. My point is this: no matter what laws Blake has broken or bent in other countries, nobody—nobody—is going to make a move against him. They're too afraid of what information Blake might leak."

"What's going to happen to all this ultrasensitive information when Blake dies?"

Insolers shrugged. "That's anybody's guess; it's not something the people at Langley like to think about. Knowing the Swiss, they'll probably move in before anybody else and confiscate the records. That's fine with the CIA, because the Swiss won't let anything in those computer records interfere with business; they might even destroy them. Anyway, I think you now have a somewhat clearer picture of the situation you're up against."

"Thank you, Insolers. Again."

"Back off on this one, Sinclair. You've already fucked him over pretty good."

"I hear what you're saying, Insolers. I appreciate the information and advice. At the moment, you're the only person who knows I have even a passing interest in Blake."

"That's arguable. From the description a few people will give the Houston police, somebody's bound to make you— which means I'm going to have to do some fast and fancy talking to my superiors, but that's not your problem. Your problem is that somebody's liable to figure out your next stop."

"If you thought you knew, would you tell?"

"Nope. After what happened at the plant, I'm going to have to figure a way to put a lot of distance between you and me in order to save my own ass."

"I understand that you can't do anything to help me attack Blake and Tommy Wing—if that's what I plan to do. Assuming I was planning to go to Geneva, would you take any steps to stop me?"

"Nobody has to try to stop you," Isolers replied without hesitation. "I think, by now, you appreciate how much respect I have for you and your skills, Sinclair. But all those skills are no match for the power Blake commands. Even a *ninja* can't get into that castle. Blake hardly ever leaves it, and he doesn't take a piss without six bodyguards around to shake his dick for him. When he does go out, he travels in a bulletproof limousine. If you think Howard Hughes was paranoid about germs, then you have some idea of how R. Edgar Blake fears assassination. And then, there's his army."

Chant rose, drained his glass, and set it down on a table beside the chair. "You're sure the woman will be all right?"

"I told you what the doctors told me," Insolers said, rising. "If you're leaving, I'll have somebody drive you to wherever it is you want to go."

"Thanks, but I'll walk."

"Walk? Christ, Sinclair, it's a mile out to the highway, and twenty miles to town."

"I can use the exercise."

"I'll drive you, if you still feel the need to have me nearby to kill."

"It's not you, Insolers. There are the doctors and nurses, and there may be monitoring devices in this house, or your cars, that you don't know about. I've already stayed here longer than I should have, and I don't want anybody to see me leave."

Insolers shrugged. "I guess if I'd been hunted for as long as you have, by as many people as you have, I'd be pretty careful, too."

Chant firmly gripped the hand that was held out to him. "The woman has earned a good deal of money working for me. I'll be opening a savings account in her name—her assumed name—at the main branch of the Houston National Bank. The President of the bank will be holding her passport. Tell her that when she's well."

Insolers frowned, studied Chant's face for some time. "That's all you want me to tell her?"

"Give her my thanks," Chant said as he headed toward the door, "and tell her I said good-bye."

CHAPTER NINETEEN _____

"IT APPEARS TO be a labyrinth, Captain—a huge one. It's probably very old, perhaps part of the original castle design, but it does show signs of upkeep."

"Any possibilities there, Sergeant?"

Alistair watched Sergeant Major Thomas McGillis as the crippled Vietnam vet looked up from the large magnifying glass Chant had been holding for him over one of a dozen blown-up aerial photographs of R. Edgar Blake's castle, which were strewn out over the surface of a large table in a back room of a friend's restaurant overlooking Lake Geneva. Since Chant had rescued his onetime sergeant from the living death of a VA hospital the man had become positively animated. Especially now that John Sinclair had brought him to Europe to help plan the assault on R. Edgar Blake's castle.

Alistair, who sat sipping a glass of wine at the table in the curtained alcove where they came every day to have lunch and talk strategy, doubted that his employer needed any help in interpreting the photographs. Indeed, Alistair had the distinct impression that John Sinclair had already decided on a plan of attack, and was using these strategy sessions as a kind of therapy for Thomas McGillis. But then, Alistair knew that nothing was ever certain with John Sinclair.

"Uncertain," the sergeant major replied at last. "You can tell that much of the area is camouflaged to prevent photos like this from being read properly. The real question is whether the castle is primarily defended from the surrounding wall and outer perimeter of the labyrinth, or at the castle walls themselves. Then, of course, there's the problem of getting through the labyrinth once the surrounding wall has been breached; the labyrinth could be mined."

"Well, these photos are as good as a map for getting through it."

"It could very well look much different on the ground, sir."

"Not a problem."

"All right, but we have to assume that the castle grounds will be laced with sensors—probably underground, impossible to detect from casual observation."

Alistair turned in his seat, pulled back the curtain over a large window, and looked down at the plaza below the restaurant. Beyond the plaza, the waters of Lake Geneva reflected the brilliant blue of a bright, clear, late-winter sky. The lake's distinctive geyser shot a hundred feet into the air, plumed, caught and broke the rays of the sun into thousands of shards of light, then rearranged them to form a luminous rainbow. In the distance, R. Edgar Blake's black stone castle sat like a stain rising up from the opposite shore.

Alistair's old but sharp eyes swept the plaza as he looked for anyone, anything, suspicious. He frowned when he saw a tall, thin man in a light overcoat standing alone in the center of the plaza, almost directly below the restaurant. The man's thin, brown hair was blowing in the stiff breeze coming off the lake, and he was shivering in the cold—an unnecessary discomfiture, Alistair thought, since there were a number of sheltered areas close by where he could stand and wait for somebody. It appeared to Alistair that the man was going out of his way to be noticed. . . .

"There's always the possibility of creating some kind of

diversion," the sergeant continued.

Chant shook his head. "No. There must be as little disturbance as possible—none that can be detected beyond the castle walls."

"Excuse me, sir," Alistair said.

Chant looked up from one of the photographs. "What is it, Alistair?"

"I'm sorry to interrupt you, Mr. Sinclair, but it looks like there might be something funny going on out there—a man, just standing there in the cold. He gives me a funny feeling."

Chant leaned across the table, pulled back the curtain a few inches, glanced down at the plaza. "You did very well, Alistair," Chant said, and immediately dropped the curtain back into place. "Sergeant, I'd like to borrow your wheelchair for a few moments, if I may."

"It's all yours, sir," the sergeant major said, raising his arms to allow Chant to lift him out. "I'm sure Alistair won't mind keeping me propped up until you get back."

"You're going to catch cold out here, Insolers."

Duane Insolers turned around at the sound of the familiar voice, found himself looking down at a crumpled figure in a wheelchair. The man wore a huge fedora, which shaded most of his face. A blanket lay over his lap, and there was no doubt in the CIA operative's mind that there was a gun under the blanket, aimed at his heart.

"I'm alone, Sinclair."

"All right."

"I knew damn well you had to be in the neighborhood, and I figured if I stood around out in the open long enough, you'd find me."

"I've found you."

"Have you figured out a way yet to get into the lion's den?"

Chant said nothing.

"I came to warn you, Sinclair," Insolers continued. "They've put together enough pieces in New York and Houston to figure out that the man in the puzzle is you. Like I told you, it wasn't hard for them, considering your MO, to guess that sooner or later you'd come here to try and off Blake. Blake's already been advised of the situation—he was just a bit pissed at what you'd done to R.E.B. and his assassination bureau, but he finds it quite amusing that you would even think of trying to get at him here."

"I would think that the CIA, not to mention the FBI and various other law enforcement agencies around the world, would be just a bit pissed at Mr. Blake."

"Oh, they are; make no mistake about it. But I've already explained *that* situation to you. All has been forgiven. You haven't even made Blake slightly nervous, Sinclair. The entire focus now is on finally capturing—and probably killing— you. There are going to be a lot of people in Geneva tomorrow—combing the city, checking passports at the airport and border checkpoints. There are also going to be snipers all over the place up in the hills surrounding that castle, rotating on eight-hour shifts, just itching to get a glimpse of you in their sights—and they won't care if it's tomorrow, or next week. They figure you're here, or somewhere else in Switzerland, planning, and they intend to simply wait for you to show up at the castle. It's time to go home, Sinclair—wherever that may be. Whatever you've been cooking up won't work now. You've run out of time. If you're not out of Switzerland by tomorrow, you may never get out."

"Have they connected you to me in Houston?"

"No. At the moment, I'm their fair-haired boy; I have them convinced I got the woman out by myself, after putting a lot of pressure on you and forcing you to blow up the place. They know we were both in there at the same time, but they don't know our paths ever crossed."

"What about the people in the safe house?"

"I'm a senior field operative. They're trained to see no evil, hear no evil, speak no evil—unless they're questioned. So far, they haven't been questioned."

"And if they are?"

"Don't worry about it."

"Why did you come to warn me, Insolers?"

"I thought I'd already explained that, Sinclair. I owe you

my life. I've always liked your choice of targets, and I think
the odds in this situation stink. You deserve better than to be
gunned down like an animal in R. Edgar Blake's front yard; it
offends my sensibilities."

"Thanks, Insolers," Chant said as he started to turn the
wheelchair. "Now I'm the one who owes you."

"I brought Jan Rawlings with me, Sinclair. We have rooms
in the Château Aumont. Do you want to see her?"

Chant swung the wheelchair back around. "Why did you
bring her?"

Insolers smiled thinly. "Jan is the most persistent and per-
suasive woman, Sinclair—as I'm sure you're well aware. She
wouldn't be denied; she says to tell you that you gave her a
job, she's not quitting, and she won't be fired." Insolers
paused, continued quietly, "She's in love with you. Maybe
you know that."

"You make a lousy matchmaker, Insolers. You never
should have brought her here."

Insolers bent over slightly in order to study the face under
the broad brim of the fedora. "I'll be damned, Sinclair," he
said after a few moments. "You love her too, don't you? It's
why you tried to leave her behind in Houston. The last thing
John Sinclair needs is to be in love with someone, or to have
someone in love with him. You know, that's almost touching."

"You shouldn't have brought her here, Insolers," Chant
repeated. "Does she know about what's coming down?"

"Yep. She adamantly believes that it doesn't make any difference at all how many men are coming, or when they come;
she says you'll still go after Blake. Is she right?"

Chant did not reply.

"Now the truce is over, Sinclair," Insolers continued
evenly. "In a little less than eight hours, I'll be just one more
man hunting John Sinclair. It has to be that way."

"I understand. Send the woman back to the United States."

"Leave Switzerland, Sinclair. Get out of here fast. Now."

"Good-bye, Insolers," Chant said, then turned the wheelchair and rolled away.

•   •   •

Alistair, who had been watching out the restaurant window as Chant talked with Duane Insolers, hurried out the back entrance as Chant left the man. He met Chant at the bottom of a ramp, took the blanket from him as Chant rose, folded the chair.

"Sir . . . ?"

"It's nothing, Alistair," Chant said, heading up the ramp and back into the restaurant.

Alistair hurried after, rearranged the blanket on Thomas McGillis's lap as his employer lifted the man back into the wheelchair.

"Alistair," Chant said, "I want you to call ahead to Zermatt and have your staff there prepare the chalet. You'll be taking the sergeant major there. I'll be along in a day or two."

"You're . . . staying here by yourself, Mr. Sinclair?"

"Yes."

Thomas McGillis glanced up quickly. "But we haven't even begun to come up with a way to penetrate the security around the castle, sir."

"Sergeant, I'm afraid planning time is over."

"But what are you going to do?"

Chant looked at the two men, smiled. "What I said I'd do: join you in Zermatt in a day or two." Then he turned and headed for the door.

CHAPTER TWENTY _____

CHANT WALKED FROM the restaurant across the plaza and hailed a taxi. After giving the driver directions, he immediately began to remove his disguise. Under the increasingly startled gaze of the driver, who kept glancing at his mysterious passenger in the rearview mirror, Chant took off his dark wig and false mustache, removed his black contact lenses. At the opposite end of the lake Chant paid the driver, got out, and casually tossed the wig and mustache into a wire trash basket on the sidewalk, along with all but two of the GTN capsules he had taken from the preparation room in the research section at R.E.B. Pharmaceuticals. The remaining two capsules he palmed, pressing them into the fleshy part of his hands between thumb and forefinger.

The grounds of R. Edgar Blake's castle were surrounded by a ten-foot-high stone wall topped with barbed wire, the entrance blocked off by a massive, wrought-iron gate. Chant walked up to the gate, pressed the brown button on the call box mounted to the right. Two tiny television cameras mounted on top of the gate swiveled around, stopped on him.

"*Qui est là?*"

"This is the big, bad wolf," Chant replied dryly. "Let me in, or I'll huff and I'll puff and I'll blow your house down."

"Go away!" the voice from the call box snapped in English. "You're drunk! Don't stay around here or you could be hurt!"

Chant looked up into the television camera directly above his head, winked. "My name is John Sinclair. I want to see Blake; go find him and tell him I'm here. I guarantee you he'll want to see me."

The call box fell silent, but both television cameras remained focused on him. Almost five minutes passed before there was the click of an electronic lock and the gate popped open an inch. There were no instructions from the box, so Chant pushed open the gate and began walking up the wide driveway to the castle. He had gone no more than twenty yards when the great wooden door that was the entrance to the castle swung open and a half dozen uniformed men, carrying Uzi submachine guns, came sprinting out. Two men continued to run down the center of the driveway directly toward him, while the others fanned out, two to a side, to cover his flanks. Chant kept walking.

"Halt!" Uwe von Deck shouted.

Chant stopped walking, casually raised his arms. All six men, automatic weapons raised, slowly converged on him until the muzzles of their guns were touching his temples, his spine, his sides. "I really hope everybody doesn't start firing at once," Chant said easily. "You'll all end up killing each other."

The leader, von Deck, slowly shook his head. In his eyes was bewilderment—and not a little regret. "What the hell are you doing here, Sinclair?"

"I was in the neighborhood, so I thought I might just pop in to say hello to your boss."

"You're a dead man, Sinclair," von Deck said, and Chant noted the ambiguity in the man's tone. "I can't imagine what the hell you were thinking of coming here."

Chant did not reply, and he stood quietly, arms still raised, as von Deck expertly searched him, running his hands over his body, emptying his pockets, feeling each seam, pulling up his pants' legs, examining his socks and the heels of his shoes. As the body search continued, Chant glanced up and saw that a number of figures—all but two in uniform—had gathered on a balcony on an upper floor of the black stone castle. There was a stooped figure in a black, woolen cape and black hat, surrounded by security guards. Hammerhead stood by himself, off to one side.

It was almost five minutes before von Deck was satisfied that Chant carried no weapons. "Keep your hands over your head, Sinclair," the commander of the guards said tersely. "All the way up. And walk slowly, at a steady pace. I had a small taste of just how quick and good you are, but there's no way you can dodge six bullets. The slightest move in the wrong direction, and you get bullets in your head and spine."

"I won't make any wrong moves, von Deck. Just take me to your leader."

With von Deck walking backward and aiming his Uzi at Chant's middle and the other five guards flanking him, Chant walked the rest of the way up the driveway, up a steep flight of stone steps and into the gaping maw of the castle. There was a cavernous foyer of carved stone carpeted with Persian rugs and hung with richly embroidered tapestries, which served to soften and warm the cold stone. A massive door to the left of the foyer opened, and Chant was ushered into a huge library with blazing fireplaces cut into all four walls. At the opposite side of the library, silhouetted by the flames in one of the walk-in fireplaces, was R. Edgar Blake, dressed in a silk lounging robe, standing just behind two guards who also carried Uzis.

The old man was pencil thin, quite tall despite his stoop, and had a full head of hair, which was still jet black. He had a long, hooked nose flanked by small, rheumy eyes. Bent slightly forward, with his hands shoved into the roomy pockets of his lounging robe, he reminded Chant of nothing so much as a vulture.

Hammerhead stood alone to Chant's right, in front of another fireplace, his scarred, misshapen face openly displaying anger and consternation. His emerald-green eyes glowed with unnatural brightness; his long, ape arms hung loose at his sides as he unconsciously flexed and unflexed his long fingers.

"Guard him well, Commander," Blake said to von Deck in a thin, breathy voice. "John Sinclair is truly *ninja.*"

"Yes, sir," von Deck replied crisply, not taking his eyes from Chant's face.

"Well, Mr. Sinclair," Blake said, rocking so far forward on the balls of his feet that his head almost came between the shoulders of the two men flanking him. "I must say this is a most unexpected and pleasant surprise. I really can't begin to imagine why you came here. Would you enlighten me?"

"It occurred to me the other day that I owe you money," Chant said easily. "Two million dollars, if I remember correctly."

In contrast to his weak speaking voice, R. Edgar Blake's laugh was raucous, high-pitched, and echoed around the stone and wood walls of the library. "Two million dollars!" he said at last, gasping for breath. "That's wonderful! I have easily spent twice that amount paying for information and hunting you. And then there is the virtual destruction of my factory in Houston, not to mention your forcing me to abandon an operation that was really quite useful to me. At the very least, I would estimate that you owe me a minimum of forty million dollars, to date, in lost property, interest, income, and general aggravation."

"Well, I'm a little strapped for cash at the moment."

Suddenly the library was absolutely still, except for the crackle of flames in the fireplaces. The old man removed the gold watch from his wrist, hefted it in his palm, looked up at Chant. When he spoke, all traces of laughter were gone from his voice and face. "You have precisely ten seconds to share with me what's on your mind before my men take you out in the back and shoot you."

"I want to retire," Chant said evenly.

Again, there was absolute silence. Except for Uwe von Deck's, all eyes in the room turned to look at the old man, hunched over, peering at his watch. Ten seconds passed, and R. Edgar Blake looked up.

"Retire?"

"Right. I think I've run out of time, Blake. If you want to hear what I have to say, I'm afraid you'll have to give me an extension."

R. Edgar Blake's response was to slip his watch into a pocket of his lounging robe.

"I'm tired, Blake," Chant continued. "I'm tired of always being hunted—by Interpol, the CIA, the United States FBI, a hundred different police organizations around the world, and especially by you."

R. Edgar Blake's thin lips pulled back from false teeth that seemed a bit too large, too bright. "Not to worry, Mr. Sinclair. I will soon cure you of this weariness from which you suffer."

Chant slowly lowered his arms. When there was no objection, he casually thrust his hands into his pockets, released the GTN capsules. "Chances are I'll be dead soon anyway, Blake," Chant said evenly. "Sooner or later, somebody who's chasing me is bound to catch up and put a bullet in my back—unless you tell them all to stop."

Again, the harsh, raucous laughter echoed through the library. "Sinclair, that is absolutely the funniest thing I've ever heard anyone say."

"You've spent a lot of time and money hunting me. Now you have me—a feat that all others have failed to accomplish in nearly twenty years of trying. The reason you now have me in your power is precisely because you are the one man in the world who can get everyone else off my back."

R, Edgar Blake studied Chant's face for some time, then slowly nodded. "So. You are not a stupid man, Sinclair. At last reports you were not insane, and you are certainly not a man to beg for mercy. I'm afraid I've been just a bit slow on the uptake. Obviously, you have come to me with a proposition which you think I'll take seriously."

"Precisely. I've heard that tough men interest you. I've also heard that you like a good show." Chant paused, pointed at Hammerhead, who was still staring intently at Chant, his face darkening. "For example, you keep Tommy Wing around as a kind of household pet—"

"Sinclair, you son-of-a-bitch, I'll kill you!" Tommy Wing shouted, and started forward.

R. Edgar Blake merely turned his head slightly in Tommy Wing's direction; Hammerhead's face paled, and he quickly stepped back to his position in front of the fireplace. "Excuse me, sir," he said quietly.

"I'm impressed, Blake," Chant said. "I've never seen anyone able to order Tommy around like that. Then again, maybe he's become too domesticated to interest you anymore. You take pride in believing you have the most savage, brutal street fighter in the world as your personal 'gofer.' I thought it might amuse you to see somebody beat him."

"You, Sinclair?" Blake's rheumy eyes took on new life behind their whitish film, gleamed. His mouth had dropped open slightly, and his breathing quickened.

"Of course. I propose, for your amusement, a fight to the death between Wing and myself, with any weapon he—or you—may choose."

"Mr. Blake, it's a trick!" Hammerhead shouted. "You don't know this bastard like I do! You can't trust him! If you take my advice, you'll shoot him right now!"

Once again, R. Edgar Blake's head turned slightly in the heavyset man's direction. "Are you afraid of Mr. Sinclair, Tommy?" he asked mildly.

"I ain't afraid of anybody, Mr. Blake," Hammerhead said, his face flushing a deep, brick red. "But I know Sinclair; he's up to something."

"Up to something?" Blake turned back to Chant. "Are you 'up to something,' Mr. Sinclair?"

"If I'm up to something besides what I just proposed, it had better be damn good, considering all the firepower you've got trained on me. I've just told you what I'm up to. If Wing kills me—then you've saved yourself a round of ammunition, and you'll be satisfied that Wing is still the matchless gutter fighter you think he is. At the least, I think I'll give him a good tussle, and you a good show. Tommy bites, you know. If *I* win, I reimburse you the two million dollars I stole from you, and you call off your dogs. You also send out word to the Americans, the British, the Mafia, Interpol, and anyone else interested in capturing or killing me that I'm no longer fair game. You will notify them that I'm going into permanent retirement, will no longer disturb anyone, and do not wish to be disturbed. You—and only you—can make them swallow that."

"You should pay me at least ten million dollars, Sinclair. Even that wouldn't begin to cover what you've cost me."

"Do I take it that we're negotiating? I'll go ten million— but you have to agree to call all the hunters off if I win, and make it stick."

"You really think I have the power to do that, Sinclair?"

"I know you do. Everybody's worried that one day you'll start leaking secrets from those extensive computer files you keep."

"My, my. You seem remarkably well informed."

"I try to keep up to date on current events. What about it, Blake? Feel like seeing a good fight?"

"What's to stop me from killing you, even if you do manage to kill Tommy?"

"Nothing—except for the fact that you wouldn't get your ten million. I mean, you may have billions, but ten million is still ten million, isn't it?"

Blake shrugged his frail shoulders. "That would be a consideration. Ten million dollars just doesn't go as far as it used to."

"Also, if you killed me after I'd won, you wouldn't have the pleasure of exercising your ego by doing for me what I've asked. Somehow, I think you'd get a big kick out of it. In any case, I really had nothing to lose by coming here to make my proposition; you're the only chance I have to see what old age is like. Right now, there are a lot of men on their way to Switzerland. I suspect the airports have already been sealed off."

"Ah, you know that, too?" Blake paused, seemed deep in thought. "When do you propose that this duel take place?"

"Whenever you'd like. If you feel up to a little excitement and bloodletting, now seems as good a time as any."

Blake turned toward Hammerhead. "Tommy, do you feel up to a little afternoon exercise?"

Hammerhead's lids were half-closed, and he was rocking back and forth, his long arms swinging like pendulums at his sides. "I'll kill him for you right now, right here, Mr. Blake. Just give me the word."

"Oh, I don't think we want to hurry things. First, we must discuss choice of weapons."

"Tommy keeps his weapons in his head," Chant said.

"And what about you, Mr. Sinclair? What would you like to fight with?"

"What would you like to see me fight with?"

"I think it would amuse me to have you look over my modest collection of weapons. Then you may choose."

"You haven't said we have a deal, Blake."

"No, I haven't, have I?" R. Edgar Blake replied mildly. "Perhaps I'll make a final decision after I see you fight. As you mentioned, you don't seem to have much to lose—and you have no choice."

Chant shrugged. "I guess you've got me."

Blake, his eyes gleaming, turned to his left and crooked a finger toward a wooden, iron-banded door next to one of the fireplaces. "I've already had lunch, and I believe I'll skip my nap for today. Let's go down to the armory."

CHAPTER TWENTY-ONE ___

CHANT, WITH THE muzzle of an Uzi pressed to the base of his skull, was ushered down a series of circular stone staircases into the depths of the castle. He carried the images of the aerial photographs in his mind, and he knew what part of the castle he wanted to get to, but he had no control of the situation. He had no choice but to go where Blake wanted him to go and hope that in his eventual duel with Hammerhead he would be afforded the opportunity he needed.

Finally they left the staircase, and Chant was led down one particularly long corridor; if his orientation had not left him, Chant was certain that they were heading toward the rear of the castle, beyond which lay the vast, ancient labyrinth.

That was where he wanted to go.

The corridor ended in a huge, circular room where the only modern feature was recessed fluorescent lighting, which filled the chamber with an eerie glow, like early-morning fog. The walls of the ancient armory were festooned with medieval weapons of various sorts, which hung from stone pegs— maces, axes, spiked clubs, swords, shields. Directly across the room from the entrance was a set of heavy wooden double doors secured in their center by a single connecting bolt.

Chant was led to the middle of the room, and then the guards—their weapons still pointed at Chant—fanned out around the walls. Hammerhead stood a few paces to Chant's left.

"Gentlemen," Blake said in his high, nasal voice, "I offer you your choice of weapons. Take your time, choose wisely, for your lives may depend on your choice. When each of you has chosen a weapon, we will repair to more suitable and spacious fighting grounds. Mr. Sinclair, I caution you not to touch any of the weapons—merely indicate what it is you want, and we will bring that weapon to the fighting ground for you."

Chant clasped his hands behind his back and took a few steps toward a wall where a mace and three broadswords were suspended.

"Stop right there, Sinclair!" von Deck barked.

"I won't touch anything," Chant said easily. "I just want to take a closer look. After all, I wouldn't want to choose something that would break over Tommy's hard head, would I?"

"That's close enough."

Chant stopped, turned his back on Hammerhead, and pretended to be studying the weapons on the walls. He had no idea where Blake intended to stage the fight, but he knew where he wanted to go—on the opposite side of the bolted doors. To get there, he needed Hammerhead's cooperation— and he was gratified when suddenly he felt Tommy Wing's long arms wrap themselves around his chest, trapping his arms; he felt Wing's hot breath as the buck teeth descended toward the back of his neck and his spinal cord, heard the man's guttural grunt of triumph.

Chant brought his head back sharply into Tommy Wing's face. Wing cried out, but his arms did not loosen their iron grip. Chant brought his heel down precisely on Hammerhead's instep with all the force of his *kai*, felt the arched bone crumple like a mound of paper. Again he brought his head back into Hammerhead's face, then slipped out of the man's loosened grip, stepped away, and turned around.

Tommy Wing, his right foot held slightly off the ground and one hand to the bleeding, pulpy mound that was his nose, was staring at Chant, disbelief in his eyes—and a flicker of fear.

"Tsk, tsk," Chant said, shaking his head. "Tommy, I think the good life has spoiled you. I remember the time when virtually no man could have gotten away from you once you'd wrapped those gorilla arms around him. I did, but it cost me a couple of cracked ribs and a big chunk of flesh out of my shoulder. But that was almost twenty years ago. Damned if I don't think you're out of practice."

"Damn you, Sinclair," Wing murmured as he tried to put weight on his right foot and winced. "Damn you."

"Come on, Tommy," Chant said casually. "I have a few other new moves to show you."

"My, my, Tommy," R. Edgar Blake said mildly. "This comes as quite a shock to me; Mr. Sinclair makes defeating you seem quite easy."

Hammerhead looked at Blake, whose eyes were fixed on Chant. Beads of perspiration had formed high on the old man's forehead. Hammerhead limped back a few steps, reached up on the wall, and took down a spiked mace and chain. Swinging the weapon in a figure-eight pattern in front of his body, he advanced on Chant.

"Sinclair," Blake said, "you have my permission to remove a weapon with which to defend yourself."

But Chant remained motionless as Hammerhead, wincing each time he stepped on his broken foot, shuffled toward him. Suddenly Wing shouted and, extending his simian arms to full length, swung the mace and leaped forward. Moving with a speed that made it virtually impossible for the others in the room to follow him, Chant spun around and stepped inside the arc of the swinging arms. The spiked iron ball crashed into the stone wall behind Chant, and by the time Hammerhead realized his mistake he was already being lifted into the air like a child, spun around, hurled through the air. His body struck the double doors, the bolt snapped, and the doors burst open.

Beyond the doors, as he had hoped, Chant could see an arched stone bridge leading to another section of the sprawling castle; below the bridge was the beginning of one of the tangled, green arms of the ancient labyrinth.

Incredibly, Tommy Wing struggled first to his knees, then to his feet, where he swayed. Blood streamed from a gash on his forehead, ran down both cheeks, joining the stream from his broken nose to drip in crimson globs off his chin. Moving very deliberately, using his peripheral vision to keep track of the men with their guns trained on him, Chant picked up the mace, walked slowly through the doors and out onto the bridge. He was not ordered to stop, and he kept walking until he was only a few paces away from the other man. The crippled Hammerhead glared at Chant, hatred blending with the pain in his eyes. Slowly, like a robot programmed to continue until self-destruction, he extended his arms, bared his teeth, and came at Chant.

"Here, Tommy," Chant said easily as he casually tossed the mace onto the stone in front of Wing. "You dropped this."

Wing, surprise on his face, snatched up the mace. Then, swinging the weapon, he began hobbling forward once again. Chant slowly backed away, angling across the width of the bridge as the spiked ball whistled through the air just inches from his face. Another two or three steps, Chant thought, and he would be up against the stone balustrade. . . .

Swing, step. Swing, step. Swing . . .

"That's far enough, Sinclair!" Uwe von Deck shouted. "Stop right there!"

But Chant had already spun around, and he vaulted easily over the balustrade to drop out of sight as bullets sang in the air above his head. He landed lightly on his feet in the center of the path between two thick, tangled walls of shrubbery. He somersaulted forward to break his fall, came up on his feet, and darted to his left through a narrow break in the green wall. Keeping low, he ran down the narrow corridor until he came to another break on his left, darted through that. There he paused, parted the shrubs a crack, and looked through, back toward the castle.

Blake and von Deck, flanked by the rest of the guards, were standing at the stone railing, leaning over and looking down at the spot thirty yards away where he had initially landed. A few moments later Hammerhead's bleeding head and torso appeared as he lurched forward, slumped on the balustrade. Blake's face was bone white, as was Hammerhead's.

"Over here!" Chant called, stepping out into the center of the path.

The submachine guns came up, swung in unison in Chant's direction.

"What's the problem, Blake?" Chant said with a shrug. "You know I'm not going anywhere, and it was your man who came at my back before you had a chance to say where you wanted us to fight. This seems as good a place as any. Send Tommy down."

"No," Blake replied tightly. "You come back up here. I can't see you fight down there, and I wouldn't want to miss any of this."

"I don't think so."

"Kill him!"

All of the Uzis opened fire simultaneously, but Chant was no longer where he had been when R. Edgar Blake had begun to issue his order. Chant had dived back through the break in the shrub wall as bullets raked through the brush around him. Almost instantly he was on his feet, crouched down and running deeper into the dark, twisted heart of the labyrinth.

When he had run fifty yards, Chant paused, still in a crouching position, and waited until the firing stopped. Then he peered through a crack, watched the assemblage behind him spread out over the span of the bridge as they scanned the maze for some sign of him. There appeared to be some heated conversation among the guards, which Chant assumed was an argument over whether or not he had been killed. Then, at a signal from Blake, everyone fell silent.

Chant watched as the old man turned to Hammerhead, who had not moved from his original position, and was still leaning on the balustrade. Blake said something, and suddenly the

guns of the guards were pointed at Hammerhead. Uwe von
Deck snapped a fresh clip of ammunition into his Uzi, then
handed the weapon to Tommy Wing, who slowly and pain-
fully hobbled down off one end of the bridge, slid down an
embankment into the labyrinth.

R. Edgar Blake cupped his hands to his mouth, shouted,
"*Sinclair?!*"

Chant remained silent.

"Sinclair!" Blake shouted again. "If you're still alive and
can hear me, I want you to know that you have no chance to
escape and come for me! Go too far into the maze, and you
will blow yourself up on a land mine! This is the only way
out, and if I wanted to I could simply post my men around this
end of the labyrinth and wait until thirst drove you out! But
I'm not going to do that! I'm sending what's left of your
opponent down to you! If you are the one to finally come out
of there, so be it! The bargain you proposed is struck! Kill
Tommy, and you'll be free to leave this castle and begin your
retirement!"

Once he had made it into the labyrinth, Chant had been
indifferent as to whether Blake sent men for him or tried to
wait him out. However, he was especially pleased that Tommy
Wing had been sent, either to retrieve his body, or to find and
kill him. Now Chant moved off to his right, keeping low,
always mindful of the watchful men on the bridge. Backtrack-
ing, using a mental image of the labyrinth gleaned from the
aerial photographs as a map, he circled around to the east. He
was certain the injured Hammerhead would take paths of least
resistance, the widest and clearest, as he wandered into the
maze; this being the case, Chant had a fairly good idea of
where Hammerhead was at the moment—and where he would
be shortly. At a juncture of corridors, Chant crouched down
behind one shrub wall and waited, half closing his eyes and
letting his vision go slightly out of focus as he probed the
depths of the maze with his hearing.

Five minutes later he heard the heavy breathing and shuffling footsteps of Tommy Wing off to his right. Chant turned,
crouched down behind the wall on the opposite side of the

path, waited. Thirty seconds later, Hammerhead—dragging his broken foot behind him and using the Uzi as a crutch—came lurching along the path.

As Hammerhead reached the juncture of the corridors, Chant abruptly stepped out in front of him. Hammerhead's eyes went wide and he opened his mouth to shout as he tried to bring the Uzi up into firing position—a fraction of a second too late, for Chant's right hand, the fingers stiff and hard as a knife blade, had already come up into his gut. Hammerhead's breath exploded from his lungs and he jackknifed forward. Chant grabbed the Uzi with his left hand, clutched the back of Hammerhead's shirt with his right, and eased the man quietly to the ground.

Chant casually rolled the doubled-over man onto his back, then reached into his pockets and took out the green capsules of GTN.

"Sweet dreams, Tommy," Chant murmured as he placed one knee on the other man's chest and dropped the capsules into the open, gasping mouth.

CHAPTER TWENTY-TWO ___

"If it's Sinclair who comes out of there," Blake said tensely, "kill him immediately."

"Yes, sir," Uwe von Deck said through lips that felt stiff.

Both men started when there was the sound of a burst of automatic-weapon fire from a section of the labyrinth to their left, perhaps two hundred yards away. Then there was silence for long minutes, finally broken by a faint shuffling sound, coming closer. There was a pause, then more shuffling. A few moments later, Tommy Wing lurched into sight in a corridor of the labyrinth below. Wing did not look up at them, but continued to stare straight ahead as he reached the end of the labyrinth, then used the Uzi in his hands as a kind of staff to help him climb the embankment to the bridge.

"Well, Tommy," R. Edgar Blake said, as surprised as von Deck to see who was emerging from the maze, "I see you've managed to come up a winner. I'm afraid there's not much of you left that would be of use to me, but I certainly give you credit for killing Sinclair—even if you did have to fill him full of bullets to do it."

Uwe von Deck frowned slightly as he watched Wing continue forward on the bridge without speaking. Something seemed wrong, von Deck thought, although he did not know what . . . unless it was the curiously vacant expression on the hobbling man's face.

"Stop him," von Deck said to his men.

Two guards immediately stepped in front of R. Edgar Blake as Hammerhead shuffled on across the bridge toward the old man. Others leaped for Wing, but they were too late to stop his long arms from swinging up and hitting the two guards in front of Blake in the chest with terrific force, knocking them backward and off their feet. Blake, his eyes wide with horror, flung up his frail arms to ward off his attacker, but Tommy Wing brushed them aside like matchsticks. Wing's long arms wrapped themselves around the old man and drew him closer. Then Wing's mouth opened and he lowered his head. . . .

Uwe von Deck sprang forward, grabbed an Uzi from one of the fallen guards. He put the muzzle of the gun directly against one of Tommy Wing's glassy green eyes and pulled the trigger. Hammerhead's head disappeared in a geyser of blood and his body slumped to the stone bridge.

Blake's head was back, and he was staring at the blue sky with unseeing eyes as blood pumped from the gaping hole in his throat where his jugular had been. Finally, he crumpled over Tommy Wing's headless corpse, twitched once, and was dead. Uwe von Deck and the other guards stared in stunned silence at the two bodies in the center of the bridge.

"Gentlemen," Chant said softly.

With the others, von Deck wheeled around, his gun aimed at the figure who had somehow mysteriously appeared behind them and was casually standing on top of the bridge balustrade. Uwe von Deck's finger tightened on the trigger of his Uzi, but he did not fire.

"Unless I'm mistaken," Chant continued matter-of-factly,

"you men are now left without gainful employment. I believe many of you will find the Swiss most unsympathetic to unemployed aliens. I suspect you'll be on your way out of the country twenty-four hours after the Swiss learn of this incident—unless, of course, something can be done to make sure you keep working. In fact, I have a proposition."

Uwe von Deck abruptly lowered his gun and flicked on the safety switch. He glanced at the others, who did the same.

"All right, Sinclair," von Deck said. "We're listening."

CHAPTER TWENTY-THREE __

JAN SAT BESIDE Duane Insolers in the passenger seat of the Mercedes-Benz that had been placed at their disposal, a smile on her face and her heart singing. The sun was just setting over Lake Geneva; in the distance, coming closer, the castle of R. Edgar Blake was uncharacteristically ablaze with light.

Grim-faced, Insolers drove through the open, unguarded gate of the castle grounds and up the wide drive to the end, where two uniformed guards were waiting for them. Insolers was not searched, which made Jan uneasy; the CIA operative had seemed very tense ever since the car and accompanying message had been delivered, and she was not at all sure what he intended to do. They were ushered into the castle, up a flight of stairs to the library.

"Chant!" Jan cried with joy when she saw the tall man with iron-colored eyes and hair standing across the room, talking with Uwe von Deck and three other guards.

"Hello, Jan," Chant said quietly, coming to her and taking her in his arms.

Jan rested her head on Chant's chest, then started and cried out when she heard the rattle of guns being raised and cocked. She quickly turned, was startled to see Duane Insolers, feet apart and braced, with both of his hands on a revolver aimed at Chant. Around the room, all of the guards stood with their guns aimed at Insolers.

"Put the gun down, Insolers," Chant said evenly as he pushed Jan away from him.

"I told you the truce was over, Sinclair."

"And I heard you; I didn't hear you tell me you were feeling suicidal."

"You're putting me into a tight box, Sinclair."

"No. Consider the fact that if you kill me, a lot of nasty secrets are going to be turned loose into the world."

Sweat appeared on Duane Insoler's face, and his jaw muscles clenched. "So you somehow managed to get to Blake and kill him," he said in a tight voice. "And now you plan to take over his operations. Already, you have these men working for you."

"Yes," Chant replied easily. "No, and no."

"What?"

"Yes, Blake's dead. No, I don't intend to have anything to do with R. Edgar Blake's operations—I have enough problems and interests of my own to keep me busy. And no, Commander von Deck and his men are not working for me."

"Then wh—?"

"Commander?" Chant said, turning to von Deck. "Who do you work for?"

"Lady Rawlings, sir," von Deck replied without taking his eyes or gun off Insolers. A smile tugged at the corners of his mouth.

"What?" Jan looked from Chant to von Deck, to Insolers. "Lady *who?*"

"Put the gun away, Insolers," Chant said. "I certainly didn't bring you here on this lovely evening so that either of us could die."

Slowly, the gun came down. "What the hell is going on, Sinclair?"

"I have a proposal for you to carry back to your people, and it's non-negotiable. Blake's computer and his files are in another wing of the castle; nobody here has checked them out—yet. Experts from the CIA and the other Western intelligence agencies will be given access and permission to destroy compromising information concerning their respective operations, past or present. As insurance, a document will be prepared, and signed by all the respective heads."

"Insurance for what?"

"The document will be held by the countess here to make sure all of you live up to your end of the bargain."

"What bargain?"

"You people are going to be doing a little rewriting of history. It seems Lady Rawlings here is R. Edgar Blake's widow, and the sole beneficiary of his estate—all of it, except for twenty million dollars the estate will be paying me for my time, trouble, and expenses. It will be up to the various intelligence agencies to come up with the necessary documents to prove that the countess now controls all of Blake's worldwide operations, as well as his fortune. Oh—I'd also appreciate it if all the men who were sent here to kill me were shipped back to wherever they came from. They can look for me some other day."

Insolers blanched. "Is that all you want?"

"That's it."

"Oh, my God," Jan whispered to no one in particular. "Oh, my God."

"It's impossible, Sinclair."

"Not for you to decide."

"They'll never go along with it."

"You could be right—in which case, newspapers around the world are going to have a field day, aren't they?"

"You'd release the information in those files?"

"Believe it—and make your superiors believe it. I understand that it will take time to untangle records, forge documents, and so on. However, the intelligence agencies have twenty-four hours to deliver a letter of intent, along with twenty million dollars for me in negotiable Swiss bonds—an advance from the CIA against the estate. If you're not back here at this time tomorrow with the letter and the bonds, the computer starts whirring and I start making calls to various news organizations to report what I'm finding out. Go, Insolers; tell them what I've told you."

"I'll deliver the message," Insolers said with a shrug, then turned and headed for the door.

"Insolers," Chant said. "Hold on; there's one more thing."

Insolers stopped, turned. "Another demand?"

Chant walked to the man, removed a manila envelope from his pocket, and handed it to the CIA operative. "Your three-grade promotion."

Insolers tore open the envelope, removed the papers from inside and read them with increasing bewilderment showing on his face. "What the *hell* is this, Sinclair?"

"It's a scenario of everything that's happened between you and me from our first meeting in New York until now. Memorize it. Jan will back up everything it says. Do you think that will impress your superiors?"

"But this isn't the way it happened at all. The Count—Jan was never your hostage, and I didn't rescue her. I never blocked anything you planned to do in New York or Houston, and I certainly didn't stop you here. This puts you in a terrible light."

Chant laughed. "Remember that I have a reputation to uphold."

Insolers slowly tore up the papers, dropped the pieces on the floor. "I don't need to slander you or consent to lies to get promoted, Sinclair."

"Suit yourself," Chant said with a shrug. "The Company could use men like you at the top."

"I'll put you in a prison cell, Sinclair. *That* would get me a promotion."

"It certainly would."

Insolers suddenly grinned. "But some other day."

"Some other day."

"Oh, my God," Jan said.

"So, Countess," Chant said, turning to Jan when Insolers had left the room. "You once told me how frustrated you were at not being able to help people as much as you wanted to. In a very few days, if I'm not mistaken, you'll control billions of dollars and a global industrial empire. I assume you'll find a few good works to do with your money and power."

Jan swallowed hard, shook her head. When she spoke, her voice squeaked. "Chant, I can't run this . . . thing. I don't have enough business knowledge—and probably not enough business sense—to run a newsstand."

"I'll send you some good advisors. Oh, by the way, I took the liberty of assuring Commander von Deck and all his men that you'd be giving them hefty raises."

"Chant, you really think the CIA and the others will *agree* to all this?"

"Yep—especially when they find out I'm involved. They'll try to pull a few stunts in the next twenty-four hours; when the stunts don't work, Insolers will show up with the letter and my money."

"I don't believe you would release those secrets."

"It depends what they are. In any case, sometimes what people believe you are, or will do, is far more important than what you actually are, or what you will actually do. They'll make the deal."

"But you won't be part of the deal," Jan said softly, her eyes misting. "Will I ever see you again?"

Chant smiled, squeezed her hand. "I wouldn't be a bit surprised. Incidentally, I have a wheelchair-bound man I'd like you to hire. For openers, I think you'll find him very useful in defusing the land mines in the labyrinth, and any other booby traps Blake has planted around this place. He can work with von Deck."

"Of course. Oh, my God."

Chant turned to von Deck. "Commander, is there anything to eat in this place?"

Uwe von Deck grinned. "There certainly is, Mr. Sinclair. In fact, I believe you and Lady Rawlings will be most impressed with the castle's food larder and wine cellar. I'll call over to the kitchen staff now and make arrangements for dinner."

"Make that dinner in two hours, Uwe," Jan said, then leaned close to Chant and whispered, "Do you suppose we can find a bedroom?"

Bestselling Thrillers —
action-packed for a great read